TT

Friday Night
in
Beast House

Friday Night
in
Beast House

Richard Laymon

headline

Copyright © 2007 Richard Laymon

The right of Richard Laymon to be identified as Author of
this work has been asserted by him in accordance with the
Copyright, Designs and Patents Act 1988.

First published in 2007
by HEADLINE PUBLISHING GROUP

1

Cataloguing in Publication Data is available from the British Library

9 780 7553 3764 4

Typeset in Janson by Avon DataSet Ltd,
Bidford on Avon, Warwickshire

Printed and bound in Great Britain by
Mackays of Chatham plc, Chatham, Kent

Headline's policy is to use papers that are natural, renewable and
recyclable products and made from wood grown in sustainable
forests. The logging and manufacturing processes are expected to
conform to the environmental regulations of the country of origin.

HEADLINE PUBLISHING GROUP
A division of Hachette Livre UK Ltd
338 Euston Road
London NW1 3BH

www.headline.co.uk
www.hodderheadline.com

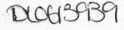

Chapter One

Mark sat on the edge of his bed and stared at the telephone.

Do it! Don't be such a wuss! Just pick it up and dial.

He'd been telling himself that very thing for more than half an hour. Still, there he sat, sweating and gazing at the phone.

Come on, man! The worst that can happen is she says no.

No, he thought. That isn't the worst. The worst is if she laughs and says, 'You must be out of your mind. What on earth would ever possess you to think I might consider going out with a complete loser like you?'

She won't say that, he told himself. Why would she? Only a real bitch would say a thing like that, and she's . . .

. . . *wonderful* . . .

To Mark, everything about Alison was wonderful. Her hair that smelled like an autumn wind. Her face, so fresh and sweet and cute that the very thought of it made Mark ache. The mischief and fire in her eyes. Her wide and friendly smile. The crooked upper tooth in front. Her rich voice and laugh. Her slender body. The jaunty bounce in her step.

He sighed.

She'll never go out with me.

But jeez, he thought, why not *ask*? It won't kill me to ask.

Before today, he never would've seriously considered it. She belonged to another realm. Though they'd been in a few classes together since starting high school, they'd rarely spoken. She'd given him a smile from time to time. A nod. A brief hello. She never had an inkling, he was sure, of how he felt about her. And he'd intended it to remain that way.

But today at the start of lunch period, Bigelow had called out, 'Beep beep!' in his usual fashion. Alison hadn't dodged him fast enough, so he'd crashed into her with his wheelchair. Down she'd gone on the hallway floor at Mark's feet, her books flying.

'Jerk!' she yelled at the fleeing Bigelow.

Mark knelt beside her. 'Creep thinks he owns the hallways,' he said. 'Are you all right?'

'Guess I'll live.'

And the way she smiled.

'Can you give me a hand?'

Taking hold of her arm, he helped her up. It was the

first time he'd ever touched her. He let go quickly so she wouldn't get the idea he liked how her arm felt.

'Thanks, Mark.'

She knows my name!

'You're welcome, Alison.'

When she stood up, she winced. She bent over, lifted the left leg of her big, loose shorts and looked at her knee. It had a reddish hue, but Mark found his eyes drawn upward to the soft tan of her thigh.

She fingered her kneecap, prodded it gently.

'Guess it's okay,' she muttered.

'You'll probably have a nice bruise.'

She made a move to pick up one of her books, but Mark said, 'Wait. I'll get 'em.' Then he gathered her scattered books and binders.

When he was done, he handed them to her and she said, 'Thanks, Mark. You're a real gentleman.'

'Glad I could help.'

He stared at the telephone.

I've *got* to call her today while it's fresh in her mind.

He wiped his sweaty hands on his jeans, reached out and picked up the phone. He heard a dial tone. His other hand trembled as he tapped in her number. Each touch made a musical note in his ear.

Before pushing the last key, he hung up fast.

I can't! I can't! God, I'm such a chickenshit yellow bastard!

This is nuts, he told himself. Calm down and do it. Hell, I'll probably just get a busy signal. Or her mom'll pick up the phone and say she isn't home. Or I'll get the answering machine. Ten to one I won't even get to talk to Alison.

He wiped his hands again, then picked up the phone and dialed . . . dialed *all* the numbers.

His arm ached to slam down the phone.

He kept it to his ear.

It's ringing!

Yeah, but nobody'll pick it up. I'll get the answering machine.

If I get the answering machine, he thought, I'll hang up.

Hang up now!

'Hello?'

Oh my God oh my God!

'Hi,' he said. 'Alison?'

'Hi.'

'It's Mark Matthews.'

'Ah. Hi, Mark.'

'I, uh, just thought I'd call and see if you're okay. How's your knee?'

'Well, I've got a bruise. But I guess I'm fine. That was really nice of you to stop and help me.'

'Oh, well . . .'

'I don't know where Bigelow gets off, going around

crashing into everybody. I mean, jeez, I'm *sorry* he's messed up and everything, but I hardly think that's any excuse for running people *over*, for godsake.'

'Yeah. It's not right.'

'Oh, well.'

There was a silence. A long silence. The sort of silence that soon leads to, 'Well, thanks for calling.'

Before that could happen, Mark said, 'So what're you doing?'

'You mean now?'

'I guess so.'

'Talking on the phone, Einstein.'

He laughed. And he pictured Alison's smile and her crooked tooth and the glint in her eyes.

'What're *you* doing?' she asked.

'The same, I guess.'

'Are you nervous?'

'Yeah.'

'You sound nervous. Your voice is shaking.'

'Oh, sorry.'

'The answer is yes.'

'Uh . . .'

'Yes, I'll go out with you.'

I can't believe this is happening!

'That's why you called, isn't it?'

'Uh, yeah. Mostly. And just to see how you're doing.'

'Doing okay. So . . . I'll go out with you.'

5

OH MY GOD!!!

'How about tomorrow night?' she suggested.

Tomorrow?

'Sure. Yeah. That'd be . . . really good.'

'On one condition,' she added.

'Sure.'

'Don't you want to hear the condition first?'

'I guess so.'

'I want you to get me into Beast House. Tomorrow night after it closes. That's where we'll have our date.'

Chapter Two

'Have you ever been in there at night?' she asked.

'Huh-uh. Have you?'

'No, but I've always wanted to. I mean, I've lived here in Malcasa my whole darn life and read the books and seen all the movies. I took the tour *before* they started using those tape players, and I know the whole audio tour by heart. I bet I know more about Beast House than most of the guides. But I've never been in there at night. It's the one thing I really want to do. I'd go on the midnight tour, but you have to be eighteen. Anyway, it's a hundred bucks apiece. And besides, I think it'd be a lot more cool going in by ourselves, don't you? Who wants to do it with a dozen other people and a guide?'

'But . . . how can we get in?'

'That's up to you. So what do you think?'

'Sure. Let's do it.'

'Where have I heard *that* before?'

He shrugged. 'I don't know, where?'

'From all the *other* guys who promised to get me in . . . and didn't.'

He felt a strange sinking sensation.

'Oh.'

'But maybe you'll be different.'

'I'll sure try.'

'I'll be at the back door at midnight.'

'Your back door?'

'The back door of Beast House. What you probably need to do is buy a ticket tomorrow afternoon and go in before it closes and find a hiding place. The thing is, they count those cassette players they give out for the tours. They can't be short a player when they go to close up for the day. If they're missing one, they know somebody's trying to stay in the house and so they search the place from top to bottom.'

'You sure know a lot about it.'

'I've studied the situation. I *really* want to spend a night in there. I think it'd be the most exciting thing I've ever done. So how about it? Are you still game?'

'Yeah!'

'All right.'

'But . . . we'll be staying in Beast House all night?'

'Most of the night, anyway. We'd have to get out before dawn.'

'Are you *allowed* to stay out all night?'

'Oh, sure. Every night.'

'Really?'

'I'm *kidding*. I'm sixteen, for cry-sake. Of course I'm not *allowed* to stay out all night. Are you?'

'No.'

'So we'll both just have to use our heads and improvise.'

'Guess so.'

'Just like *you'll* have to improvise on getting in.'

'How am I supposed to do that thing with the cassette players?'

'Where there's a will, there's a way.'

'But . . .'

'Mark, this is a test. A test of your brains, imagination and commitment to a task. I think you're a cool guy, but the world's full of cool guys. The question is, are you *worthy* of me.'

Though she sounded serious, Mark imagined her on the other phone, grinning, a spark of mischief in her eyes.

'See you tomorrow at midnight,' he said.

'I sure hope so.'

'I'll be there. Don't worry.'

'Okay. That'll be really neat if you can do it. Thanks for calling, Mark.'

'Well . . .'

'Bye-bye.'

''Bye.'

After hanging up, Mark sprawled on his bed and stared at the ceiling. Stunned that Alison had agreed to go out with him. Trembling at the prospect of being with her tomorrow night... *all* night. Slightly depressed that she seemed less interested in going out with him than in getting into Beast House. And dumbfounded by the task of how to deal with the cassette-player problem.

Where there's a will, there's a way.

Usually true, but certainly not always. He could *will* himself to flap his arms and fly to Singapore, for instance, but that wouldn't make it happen.

He'd taken the Beast House tour often enough to understand the system. They gave you a player as you entered the grounds. You wore it by a strap around your neck and listened to the 'self-guided tour' through head-phones as you walked through the house. Afterwards, you handed back the player and headphones at the front gate. Handed it *to* a staff member.

The crux of the problem, he thought, is the staff member.

Usually they were good-looking gals in those cute uniforms that made them all look like park rangers.

If nobody was watching, you could just walk up to the gate, return the audio equipment (slip it into the numbered cubbyhole in the storage cabinet), then turn around and go back to the house and find a hiding place.

Or have an accomplice drop off *both* players on his way out while you remain in the house.

But there *is* a gal at the gate and you've gotta *hand* her the player. They want to make very sure nobody's in the house when they shut it down for the night.

So how can I do it? Mark wondered. There must be a way.

It's just a matter of *thinking* of it.

Bribe the girl at the gate?

Create a diversion?

He lay there staring at the ceiling of his bedroom, trying to come up with a plan that might work. Might work when you're just a regular sixteen-year-old real kid, not Indiana Jones or James Bond or Batman.

He came up with ideas. His only good ideas, however, involved the use of an accomplice.

I've gotta do this on my own, he thought. If I drag Vick or someone into it, they might screw up the whole deal.

So he kept on thinking. The thoughts filled his head, cluttered it, whirled, bumped into each other. They didn't make his head *hurt*, but they certainly made it feel heavy and useless.

Without realizing it, he fell asleep.

He woke up at the sound of his father's voice calling from downstairs. 'Mark! You better get down here fast!

Supper's on the table. Come on, man. Move it. *Arriba! Arriba! Andalé!'*

On his way down the staircase, breathing deeply of the aroma of fried chicken, he heard a gruff Mexican voice in his head. It said, 'Tape players? We don't need no steeenkin' tape players!'

He grinned.

Chapter Three

Plans and hopes and fears swirling through his mind, Mark lay awake most of the night. But he must've fallen asleep somewhere along the line because his alarm clock woke him at seven in the morning.

Friday morning.

He lay there, staring at the ceiling, trembling.

I don't *have* to go through with it, he thought.

Oh yes I do. I've gotta. If I screw up, that'll be it with me and Alison.

But what if I get caught?

What if I get killed?

What if *she* gets killed?

By now, these were old, familiar thoughts. He'd gone through them all, again and again, while trying to fall asleep. He was tired of them. Besides, they always led to the same conclusion: getting a chance to be with Alison tonight would be worth any risk.

He struggled out of bed and staggered into the bathroom. There, he took his regular morning shower.

Afterward, instead of getting dressed for school, he put on his pajamas and robe and slippers. Then he headed downstairs.

By the time he entered the kitchen, his father had already left for work and his mother was sitting at the breakfast table with a cup of coffee and the morning newspaper. She lowered the newspaper. And frowned. 'Are you feeling all right?'

He grimaced. 'I don't think so.'

She looked worried. 'What's the matter, honey?'

'Just . . . a pretty bad headache. No big deal.'

'Looks like you're not planning on school.'

'I *could* go, but . . . we never do much on Fridays anyway. Most of the teachers just show movies or give us study time. So I guess, yeah, it'd be nice to stay home. If it's okay with you.'

He knew what the answer would be. He made straight A's, he'd never gotten into any trouble and he rarely missed a day of school. The few times he'd complained of illness, his mother had been perfectly happy to let him stay home.

'Sure,' she told him. 'I'll call the attendance office soon as I'm done with my coffee.'

'Thanks. I guess I'll head on back to bed.'

As he turned away, his mother said, 'Will you be okay by yourself? This is my day to work at the hospital.'

'Oh, yeah, that's right.' He'd known full well that she worked as a volunteer at the hospital every Friday. It was perfect. Many of her regular activities kept her in town, but not this one. For the privilege of doing volunteer work in the hospital gift shop, she had to drive all the way to Bodega Bay. More than an hour away. She would have to leave very soon. And she wouldn't be getting home until about six.

By then, Mark thought, I'll be long gone.

'I'll be fine by myself,' he said.

Frowning, she said, 'I'll be gone all day, you know.'

'It's no problem.'

'Maybe I should call one of the other girls and see if I can't find someone to fill in for me.'

'No, no. Don't do that. There's no point. I'll be fine. Really.'

'Are you sure?'

'I'm sure. Really.'

'Well . . . I'll be home in time to make dinner. Or maybe I'll pick up something on the way back. Anyway, why don't you make yourself a sandwich for lunch? There's plenty of lunchmeat and cheese in the fridge . . .'

'I know. I'll take care of it. Don't worry.'

Upstairs, he took off his robe and slippers and climbed into bed. He lay there, gazing at the ceiling, trembling, trying to focus on his plans but mostly daydreaming about Alison.

After a while, his mother came to his room. 'How are you doing, honey?'

'Not bad. I'll be fine. I took some aspirin. I probably just need some sleep.'

'You sure you don't want me to stay home?'

'I'm sure. Really. I'll be fine.'

'Okay then.' She bent over, gave him a soft kiss on the cheek, then stood up. 'If you start feeling worse or anything, give me a call.'

'I will.'

She nodded, smiled and said, 'Be good.'

'I will. You, too.'

She walked out of his room. A few minutes later, he heard her leave the house. He climbed out of bed. Standing at his window, he watched her drive away.

Then he went to his desk, took a sheet of lined paper from one of his notebooks and wrote:

Dear Mom and Dad,
I'm very sorry to upset you, but I had to go someplace tonight. I'll be back in the morning. Nothing is wrong. Please don't worry too much or be too angry at me. I'm not upset or nuts or anything. This is just something I really want to

do, but I know you wouldn't approve or give permission.

Love,
Mark

He folded the note in half and put it on his nightstand. After making his bed, he got dressed. He'd thought a lot about what to wear and what to take with him.

Down in the kitchen, he made two ham-and-cheese sandwiches. He put them into baggies and slipped them into his belly-pack. He added a can of Pepsi from the refrigerator. Realizing its condensation would make everything else wet, he took it out, put it inside a plastic bag, then returned it to his pack.

In the kitchen 'junk drawer', he found a couple of fair-sized pink candles. He put them, along with a handful of match books, into his pack. After fitting his Walkman headphones into the pack, there was no room left for the Walkman itself.

I don't need it anyway.

He put on his windbreaker, then glanced at the digital clock on the oven.

8:06.

Perfect.

Patting the pockets of his jeans, he felt his wallet, comb, handkerchief and keys.

That should do it.

He looked around, wondering if he was forgetting anything.

Yeah, my brains.

He grinned.

Chapter Four

Outside the house, he took a deep breath and filled himself with the cool, moist scents of the foggy morning.

A wonderful morning, made for adventure.

He trotted down the porch stairs and headed for Front Street.

In the early stages of making plans, he'd considered trying to sneak out of the neighborhood to avoid being spotted by friends of his parents. Friends who would blab. After a while, however, he'd realized there was no point. He might be able to sneak into Beast House and keep his rendezvous with Alison, but his parents were certain to discover his absence from home tonight. Thus, the note.

And thus, no need for sneakiness. Not here and now, anyway.

They're gonna kill me, he thought.

But not till after my night with Alison.

And if something goes wrong and I can't make it into Beast House, I'll just come home and destroy the note and nobody'll ever know what I almost did.

That might not be so bad, he thought.

It'd be *awful*! I've *got* to get into the house and be there at midnight.

Walking along, he thought about how surprised Alison would be when he opened the back door for her.

'My God!' she would say, 'you really *did* it!'

And then she would throw her arms around him, hug him with amazement and delight.

Would that be a good time to kiss her? he wondered.

Probably not. You don't go around kissing a girl at the *start* of a date. Especially if you've never gone out with her before. You've got to lead up to it, wait until the mood is just right.

We'll have *hours* together. Plenty of time for one thing to lead to another.

At Front Street, Mark stopped and looked both ways. Only a few cars were in sight, none near enough to worry about. He hurried to the other side and continued walking east for another block. The barber shop was already open, but he didn't glance in. The candle shop hadn't opened yet. Neither had Christiansen Real Estate or the Book Nook or most of the other businesses along both sides of the road. Generally, not much was open in Malcasa Point before 10:00 a.m., probably because that was when the first tour buses arrived for Beast House.

Coming to the corner, he turned right. Though bordered by businesses, the road was empty and quiet. He followed its sidewalk southward. Because of curves and low slopes, he couldn't see where it stopped. The DEAD END sign and the fence and rear grounds of Beast House wouldn't come into view for another couple of minutes.

Almost there.

Then the fun starts, he thought.

But the fun started early.

Two blocks ahead of Mark, a police car came around a bend in the road.

Oh, shit!

Just act normal!

Trying not to change his pace or the look on his face, he turned his head slightly to the right as if mildly interested in a window display.

Mannequins in skimpy lingerie.

Terrific, he thought. The cop'll think I'm a pervert.

Looking forward, he started to bob his head slightly as if he had a tune going through it.

Just a normal guy out for a walk.

He glanced toward the other side of the road.

In his peripheral vision, he saw the patrol car coming closer.

He turned his gaze to the sidewalk directly in front of him.

The cop'll get suspicious if I avoid his eyes!

Trying to seem *very* casual, still bobbing his head just a bit, he glanced at the cop. He planned to cast the officer a friendly, uninterested smile then look away, but couldn't.

Holy shit!

In the driver's seat of the police car sat the most beautiful woman in town – and by far the most dangerous – Officer Eve Chaney.

I thought she worked nights!

Heart thudding, Mark gaped at her. Though he'd seen Officer Chaney a few times at night and admired her photo in the newspaper every so often, this was his first good view of her in daylight.

My God, he thought.

She turned her head and stared straight back at him as she slowly drove by.

'Hi,' he mouthed, but no sound came from his mouth.

She narrowed her eyes, nodded, and kept on driving.

Face forward, Mark kept on walking. His face felt hot. He was breathing quickly, his heart thumping.

How'd you like to spend the night in Beast House with HER?

The prospect of that was frightening but incredibly exciting.

He suddenly felt guilty.

Hearing a car behind him, he looked over his shoulder.

Oh, jeez, here she comes!

She drove slowly, swung to the curb and stopped adjacent to him. Her passenger window glided down. Mark bent his knees slightly and peered in.

Beckoning him with one hand, Officer Chaney said, 'Would you like to step over here for a moment?'

'Me?'

She nodded.

Heart clumping hard and fast, Mark walked up to her passenger door, bent over and looked in.

He'd never been this close to such a beautiful woman.

But she's a cop and I'm in trouble.

He could hardly breathe.

'What's your name?' she asked.

'Mark. Mark Matthews.'

'I'm Officer Chaney, Mark.'

He nodded.

Though this was October, Officer Chaney made him think of summer days at the beach. Her short hair was blowing slightly in the breeze that came in through the open windows of her patrol car. Her eyes were deep blue like a cloudless July sky. Her face was lightly tanned. The scent of her, mixed with the moist coolness of the fog, was like suntan oil

'How old are you, Mark?'

He considered lying, but knew it was useless. 'Sixteen.'

She nodded as if she'd already known. 'Shouldn't you be in school?'

'I guess so. I mean, I guess it all depends.'

'How's that?'

'My mom called in sick.'

'Your mother's ill?'

'No. I mean, she called in sick for me. So I'm officially absent today.'

Officer Chaney turned slightly toward him, rested her right elbow on top of the seatback, and smiled with just one side of her mouth. Mark supposed it would be called a smirk. But it sure looked good on her. 'So you're staying home sick today?'

'That's right, officer.'

'In that case, shouldn't you be home in bed?'

'Well . . .'

He felt his gaze being pulled down to her throat, to the open neck of her uniform blouse, on a course that would soon lead to her chest. He forced his eyes upward, tried to lock them on her face.

'Well?' she asked.

I can't lie to her. She'll see right through it!

'The thing is, I'm not all that sick. And I'm a really good student anyway and Fridays at school are always pretty much of a waste of time and it's such a nice morning with the fog and all.' He shrugged.

Eyes narrowing slightly, she nodded. Then she said, 'And there are such few and such morning songs.'

Mark raised his eyebrows.

' "Fern Hill",' she said. 'Dylan Thomas.'

'Oh. Yeah. The guy who wrote "A Child's Christmas in Wales".'

This time, she smiled with both sides of her mouth. She nodded again and said, 'Have a good day, Mark.'

'Thank you, Officer Chaney. You, too.'

She looked away from him, so he quickly glanced at the taut front of her blouse before she took her arm off the seatback. Facing forward, she put both hands on the steering wheel.

Mark took a step backward but remained bent over.

Just when he expected her to pull away, she turned her head again. 'Don't do anything I wouldn't,' she told him.

'I won't. Thanks.'

She gave him another nod, then drove slowly away.

Standing up straight, Mark watched her car move down the road, watched it turn right and disappear.

'Wow,' he whispered.

Chapter Five

When Mark resumed walking, his legs felt soft and shaky. He seemed to be trembling all over.

He could hardly believe that he'd actually been stopped by Officer Eve Chaney, that he'd gotten such a good look at her. It was almost like something too good to be true. But even better – and more unbelievable – she hadn't balled him out, hadn't lectured him, hadn't busted him or driven him back to school or back to his house. She'd not only been friendly, but she had *let him go*.

Let him go with the caution, 'Don't do anything I wouldn't.'

What was *that* supposed to mean?

He knew it was just a saying. But it didn't really make a lot of sense when you considered that he didn't know enough about Officer Chaney to judge what she might or might not do. All he knew for sure was that she was a local legend. Since coming to Malcasa Point about three years ago, she'd made a lot of arrests and she'd even been in gunfights. She'd shot half a dozen bad guys, killing a couple of them.

Don't do anything I wouldn't?

'Good one,' he said quietly, and grinned.

Still shocked and amazed but feeling somewhat more calm, Mark came to the corner. He turned his head and looked toward Front Street, hoping to see Officer Chaney's car again. But it was gone.

He shook his head.

Continuing across the street, he found himself wishing that she *hadn't* let him go. If she'd busted him, he would've gotten to sit in the car with her. He would've had a lot more time to be with her.

Maybe she would've frisked me.

'Oh, man,' he murmured.

But he supposed it was just as well that she'd let him go. Nice as it might've been, it would've wrecked his plans for sneaking into Beast House. He still wanted to go through with that, or at least give it a good try – even though Alison suddenly seemed a little less special than usual.

It's just temporary, he thought. Like sun blindness. After I've been away from Officer Chaney for a while, it'll all go back to normal.

'Eve,' he said quietly. 'Eve Chaney.'

He sighed.

Hell, he thought. If Alison's out of my league (and

she is), then what's Eve? Like a grown-up, improved version of Alison, and probably at least ten years older than me. Not a chance, not a chance. The best I can ever hope for is a little look and a little talk. With Eve, it'll probably never be better than what just happened.

Forget about her.

Yeah, sure.

He suddenly found himself only a few strides away from the dead-end barricade. A little surprised, he turned around. Nobody seemed to be nearby, so he waded into the weeds, descended one side of a shallow ditch, climbed the other side, and trudged through more weeds until he stood at the black iron fence.

Beyond it were the rear grounds: the snack stand; the outdoor eating area with chairs upside-down on table tops; the restroom/gift-shop building; and the back of Beast House itself.

He saw nobody.

The parking lot, off in the distance, looked empty.

Now or never, he thought.

After another quick look around, he leapt, caught the fence's upper crossbar with both hands and pulled himself up. The effort suddenly reminded him of gym class.

He struggled high enough to chin the crossbar, then hung there, wondering what to do next. He tried to go higher, couldn't. He tried to swing a leg up high enough to catch the crossbar with his foot, couldn't.

Muttering a curse, he lowered himself to the ground. *There's gotta be a way!*

The rear side of the fence, extending along the eastern border of the lawn at the base of a hillside, was overhung in a few places by the limbs of trees outside the fence. Maybe he could climb one of the trees, crawl out on a limb to get past the fence, and drop inside the perimeter.

The limbs looked awfully high.

Climbing high enough to reach any of them might be tough. And if he succeeded, the drop to the ground . . .

He murmured, 'Shit.'

If only I'd brought a rope, he thought. I could rappel down. If only I knew how to rappel.

Screw a rope, I should've brought a ladder.

He'd heard that there were places where you could crawl *under* the fence, but he had no idea where to look for them.

There were also supposed to be 'beast holes' in the hillside . . . openings that led to a network of tunnels. But he didn't know anyone who'd ever actually *found* one.

If only I'd brought a shovel, he thought. I could dig my way under the fence.

If I'd had a little more time to prepare . . .

I've gotta get in somehow! And fast!

He glanced at his wristwatch. Ten till nine. By nine-thirty, the staff would start arriving.

He sighed, then hurried back to the street and broke into a run.

The last resort.

He'd intended to hop over the fence. While planning the details of his adventure, it hadn't seemed like such an impossible task. He'd seen people do that sort of thing all the time on TV, in movies, even in documentaries.

James Bond, he thought as he ran, would've hurled himself right over the top of a simple little fence like that.

Shit, Bond would've *parachuted* in.

As Mark ran, he realized that the *real* people he'd observed performing such feats in documentaries were Marines, Navy Seals, Army Rangers . . . not a sixteen-year-old high-school kid whose idea of a good time was reading John D. MacDonald paperbacks.

What would Travis McGee do?

The fence would've been a cinch for Travis. But he might do what I'm gonna do.

The new plan was risky. He'd kept it in the back of his mind only as a last resort.

If all else fails . . .

All else *had*.

31

Nearing the front corner of the fence, Mark slowed his pace from a sprint to a jog.

If anybody's watching, he thought, they'll think I'm just running for exercise.

A car went by on Front Street. He glanced at it, saw the driver, didn't recognize him. A moment later, the car was gone and he found himself staring at the Kutch house in the field across the street.

The sight of the old brick house sent a chill racing up his back. He knew what had happened there. And he couldn't help but wonder what might *still* be happening within its windowless walls.

Old lady Kutch lived in there like some sort of mad hermit.

There were rumors of beasts.

Of course, there were *always* rumors of beasts.

The real things were probably long gone or all killed off.

But old Agnes Kutch was beast enough for Mark. Walking too close to her house late at night, he'd once heard an outcry . . . almost like a scream, but it might've been something else.

He looked away from the Kutch house and watched Beast House as he ran toward its ticket booth.

Blood baths had taken place inside Beast House. Men, women and children had been torn apart within its walls. But the place didn't seem nearly as creepy to him as the Kutch house. Maybe because he'd been inside it so many times before. Maybe because it was flooded with tourists day after day.

Looking at the old Victorian house as he ran alongside its fence, the place seemed almost friendly.

He slowed down as he neared the ticket booth.

Looked around.

Saw a car in the distance, but it was still a few blocks away.

He walked casually to the waist-high turnstile and climbed over it.

Easy as pie.

On his right was the cupboard where the cassette players were stored. It had a padlock on it.

He walked past the cupboard, stepped around the back of the ticket shack, took a deep breath, then raced for the northwest corner of Beast House.

Chapter Six

In the area behind the house, Mark found several metal trash cans, one just to the left of the gift shop's entrance. He dragged it a few inches closer to the wall, then climbed onto it. Touching the wall for support, he rose from his knees to his feet and stood up straight.

His head was only slightly lower than the roof.

This I can do, he thought.

He sure hoped so, anyway.

Not with the belly pack on.

Releasing the wall, he used both hands to unfasten its belt. Then he put one hand on the wall to steady himself. With the other, he tossed his small pack onto the roof. It landed out of sight with a quiet thump.

Now I *have* to get up there, he thought.

Hands on the roof, he leaped, thrust himself upward and forward and imagined his balance shifting, saw himself falling backward. But a moment later, he was scurrying and writhing, digging at the tarpaper with his elbows and then with his knees until he found himself sprawled breathless.

Made it!

He raised his head. His belly pack was within easy reach. The roof stretching out ahead of him had only a slight slope. A few vent pipes jutted up here and there. Near the middle was the large gray block of the air-conditioning unit, nearly the size of a refrigerator.

He picked up his pack, crawled over to the air-conditioner and lay down beside it. Braced on his elbows, he looked around.

Nobody should be able to spot him from the ground. Anyone on the hillside would be able to see him, but people mostly stayed away from there. His main problem would be the back windows of Beast House itself, especially the upstairs windows. The air-conditioner would do a fair job of concealing him, but not a *complete* job.

He was lucky to have the air-conditioner. He hadn't known it would be here. Making his plans, however, he'd figured that the roof of the gift shop might be the only hiding place available to him.

He'd never intended to stay here all day, anyway.

He lowered his face against his crossed arms. Eyes shut, he tried to concentrate on his plans, but his mind kept drifting back to his encounter with Officer Chaney.

He told himself to stop that. If he wanted to daydream he should daydream about Alison.

He imagined himself opening the back door of Beast House at midnight, Alison standing there in the moonlight. 'You *did* it!' she blurts.

'Of course.'

'I'm so proud of you.' She puts her arms around him.

Some time later, Mark heard voices that weren't in his head.

He lay motionless.

Just a couple of voices, then more. Some male, some female. He couldn't make out much of what was being said, but supposed the voices must belong to the guides and other workers.

Soon, they seemed to hold a meeting. After a few minutes, it broke up and the voices diminished.

By the sounds of jingling keys and opening doors, he guessed that people were opening the snack stand, the restrooms and gift shop.

Mark raised his face off his arms and looked at his wristwatch.

9:55.

In five more minutes, the first tourists would start heading down the walkway to the front of Beast House. They would be stopping at Station One to hear about Gus Goucher, then entering the house and going into the parlor for Ethel Hughes's story. Then upstairs.

There, the earlier portions of the tour took place in areas toward the front of the house. Not until the boys' room would there be a window with a good view of the rear grounds.

The first tourists probably wouldn't reach the boys' room until about 10:30.

Making his plans, Mark had figured that he ought to be safe on the gift shop's roof until then.

Might be pushing it, he thought.

After all, the tour's self-guided. He'd done it often enough to know that some visitors were more interested in seeing the crime scenes and gory displays than in listening to the whole story, so they pretty much ignored the audio tape and hurried from room to room.

Only one way to be *sure* nobody saw him from an upstairs windows: get off the roof as soon after ten o'clock as possible. But he didn't want to leave his hiding place *too* early; he needed others to be around so he could mingle with them.

So he waited until ten past ten. Then he belly-crawled around the air-conditioner and saw the dog.

His mouth fell open.

The dog, big as a German shepherd, lay on its side a few feet from the far corner of the roof. It looked as if it had been mauled by wild animals. *Hungry* wild animals that had disembowelled it, torn huge chunks from its body . . .

Where's it's head? Mark wondered. Did they *eat* its head?

How the hell did it get on the roof?

Feeling a little sick, he belly-crawled toward the remains of the dog. He didn't want to get any closer, but it lay between him and the corner of roof where he needed to descend.

Flies were buzzing around the carcass. It looked very fresh, though, its blood still red and wet.

Must've *just* happened, Mark thought. Not too long before I got here. If I'd shown up a little earlier . . .

His skin went prickly with goosebumps.

There didn't seem to be a great deal of blood on the roof under and around the dog.

This isn't where the thing got nailed, Mark thought. It must've been hurled up here afterward. Or dropped?

He found his head turning toward Beast House, tilting back, his gaze moving from the second-floor windows to the roof.

Nah.

A bear could've done something like this, maybe. Or a wildcat. Or a man. A very strong, demented man.

Suddenly wanting badly to be off the roof, Mark scurried the rest of the way to its edge. He peered down. Nothing behind the building except for a patch of lawn and the back of Beast House.

For now, nobody was in sight.

Mark swung his legs over the edge. As they dangled, he lowered himself until he was hanging by his hands. Then he let go and dropped. Dropped farther than he really expected.

His feet hit the ground hard. Knees folding, he stumbled backward and landed hard on his rump.

It hurt, but he didn't cry out.

Seated on the grass, he looked around.

Nobody in sight.

So he got to his feet and rubbed his butt. Walking casually toward the far back corner of Beast House, he removed the Walkman headphones from his belly pack.

By the time he arrived at the front of the house, he was wearing the headphones. The cord vanished under the zippered front of his windbreaker, where it was connected to nothing at all.

At least a dozen tourists were milling about the front lawn or gathered in front of the porch stairs. They all wore headphones, too. Not exactly like his, but close enough.

Mark wandered over and joined those at the foot of the stairs.

He stared up at the hanged body of Gus Goucher.

He'd seen Gus plenty of times before: the bulging eyes, the black and swollen tongue sticking out of his mouth, the way his head was tilted to the right at such a nasty angle – worst of all, the way his neck was two or three times longer than it should've been.

They stretched his neck, all right.

The sight of Gus usually bothered Mark, but not so much this morning. As gruesome as it looked, it seemed bland compared to the actual remains of the dog he'd just seen.

Gus looked *good* compared to the dog.

Gazing up at the body, Mark stood motionless as if concentrating on the voice from his self-guided tour tape.

A breeze made the body swing slightly. Near Mark, a woman groaned. A white-haired man in a plaid shirt was shaking his head slowly as if appalled by Gus or the story on the tape. A teenaged girl was gaping up at Gus, her mouth drooping open.

She didn't look familiar.

None of the people looked familiar.

Not surprising. Though plenty of townies did the tour, the vast majority of visitors came from out of town, many of them brought here on the bus from San Francisco.

Several of the nearby people, including the teenaged girl, clicked off their tape players and moved toward the stairs.

Mark followed them.

Up the porch stairs, past the dangling body of Gus

Goucher, across the porch and through the front door of Beast House.

I'm in!

Chapter Seven

From now on, *staying* in would be the trick. To manage that, Mark needed a hiding place.

He glanced at the guide in the foyer. A heavy-set brunette. Busy answering someone's question, she didn't notice him. He followed a few people into the parlor.

Though not here for the tour, he figured he should *look* as if he were, and try to blend in with the others. Besides, he really liked the parlor exhibit.

Ethel Hughes, or at least her wonderfully life-like mannequin, was a babe. On the other side of a thick red cordon, she lay sprawled on the floor, one leg raised with her foot resting on the cushion. She was supposedly the first victim on the night of August 2, 1903, when the beast came up from the cellar and tried to slaughter everyone in the house. It had ripped her up pretty good. Better yet, it had ripped up her nightgown.

The replica of her nightgown, shredded in precise accordance with damage to the tattered original (now on display in Janet Crogan's Beast House Museum on

Front Street), draped Ethel's body here and there but left much of it bare. For the sake of decency, narrow strips of the fabric concealed her nipples and a wider swath passed between her parted thighs. Otherwise, she was nearly naked.

A year ago, taking the tour by himself, Mark had noticed that one of the strips was out of place just enough to let him see a pink, curved edge of Ethel's left areola. He'd gazed at it for a long time.

Today, nothing showed that shouldn't. He found himself staring at Ethel, anyway. So beautiful. And almost naked. What if a wind should come along . . .?

How? The windows are shut.

Cut it out, he thought. She's nothing compared to Alison or Officer Chaney. She's not even real.

But she sure looked exciting down on the floor like that.

The image returned to his mind of the day he'd seen Ethel with the shred of cloth off-kilter.

Quit it, he told himself.

Only one thing mattered: hiding.

Late last night in his bedroom, Mark had pulled out his copy of Janice Crogan's second book, *Savage Times*. In addition to containing the full story of Beast House, along with copies of photos and news articles, it provided floor plans of the house. He'd studied the plans, used them to refresh his memory of what he'd observed during the tours, and searched them for good a place to hide.

So many possibilities.

Behind the couch in the parlor? Under one of the upstairs beds? In a closet? Maybe. But those were so obvious. For all Mark knew, they might be routinely checked before closing time.

He needed someplace more unusual.

The attic seemed like a good possibility. Though visitors weren't allowed up there, its doors were kept open during the day. He'd heard that it was cluttered with old furniture, even some mannequins that had once been on display. He could probably hide among them until closing time ... if he could get into the attic unseen.

That would be the hard part. A guide was usually posted in the hallway just outside the second-floor entrance. And even if he should find the door briefly unguarded (maybe if he created a diversion to draw the guide elsewhere), he would hardly stand a chance of making it all the way to the top before being spotted.

I'll at least go upstairs and check it out, he thought. The attic would sure be better than the alternative.

After giving Ethel a final, lingering gaze, Mark turned around and stepped out of the parlor. The heavy-set guide was keeping an eye on people, but paid him no special attention. He turned away from her and started to climb the stairs.

Halfway up, someone behind him said, 'Is this fuckin' cool, or what?'

He looked back.

The wiry guy who'd spoken, a couple of stairs below Mark, was maybe twenty years old, had wild eyes and a big, lopsided grin. He wore his headphones over the top of a battered green Jets cap.

'Pretty cool,' Mark agreed.

'It's fuckin' bullshit, y'know. I know bullshit when I see it. But it's fuckin' *cool* bullshit, know what I mean?'

'Yeah. It's cool, all right.'

'Beast my fuckin' ass.'

'You don't think a beast did this stuff?'

'Do *you*?'

'I don't know.'

'Only one sorta beast does this sorta shit – *homo-fuckin'-sapien*.'

'Maybe so,' Mark said.

At the top of the stairs, he joined several people who'd stopped at Station Three. Reaching down inside the zippered front of his windbreaker, he pretended to turn on his tape player.

The guy from the stairs knuckled him in the arm.

'Love this Maggie Kutch shit,' he said. 'Man, she must've been fruitier than fuckin' Florida.'

Mark nodded.

'Name's Joe,' the guy said. 'After Broadway Joe, not that fuckin' twat in *Little Women*.' He cackled.

'I'm Mark.'

'Biblical Mark or question mark?'

Mark shrugged.

'First time?'

'In Beast House? No, I've been here a few times.'

'Where you from'

'Here in town.'

'I came up from Boleta Bay. I gotta come up and do the house two, three times a year. It's like I'm fuckin' addicted, man. I stay away too long, it's like my head's gonna blow up like fuckin' Mount St. Helen.'

Mark nodded again, then turned his face away and pretended to listen to his audio tour.

Beside him, Joe's player clicked on.

Around him, people were starting to move toward Lilly Thorn's bedroom. He heard a faint, tinny voice from Joe's headset. Though he couldn't make out the words, he knew they came from Janice Crogan and he knew what she was saying.

. . . *After finishing its brutal attack on Ethel, the beast ran out of the parlor and scurried up the stairs, leaving a trail of blood* . . .

She then gave instructions to leave the player on and

follow the replica blood tracks into Lilly Thorn's bedroom.

Joe turned toward Lilly's room, looked down at the tracks on the hardwood floor and smirked at Mark. 'Bloody footprints,' he said. 'I fuckin' love it.'

Mark walked beside him into Lilly's room. About a dozen other people were already inside, listening to their headphones and staring at the exhibit.

Behind the red cordon, a wax dummy of Lilly Thorn was sitting up in bed. Unlike Ethel, Lilly looked alive and terrified. This was how she might've appeared immediately after being awakened by the noise of the beast's attack on Ethel. Soon afterward, she had blocked her bedroom door shut and escaped through a window . . . surviving . . . but leaving her two small boys behind to be raped and murdered by the beast.

Joe chuckled and muttered, 'Fuckin' pussy,' in response to something he heard on the tape.

What if he STAYS with me?

He won't, Mark thought. He's just doing the tour.

Let's just see . . .

Mark turned around and took a step toward the bedroom door. Joe grabbed his arm. 'You gotta listen to the spiel, man.'

'I've heard it before. Lots of times.'

'Yeah, me too. But you know what, you get new stuff every time.'

48

Mark shook his head. 'It's always the same.'

'Yeah, the *words*. But not *you*. Every time you hear 'em, you're a different dude so they *mean* different stuff. You pick up new shit, know what I mean?'

'I guess so.'

'So you gotta listen to the whole thing, *really* listen. Got it?'

'Got it.'

Joe let go of his arm.

Mark, nodding, reached down inside his windbreaker and pretended to turn on his tape player again.

Chapter Eight

He's just hanging out with me during the tour, Mark told himself. All I have to do is walk through it with him, then he'll go his way and I'll go mine.

Maybe.

Or maybe he'll say we should have some lunch together or why not take a walk down Front Street and have a look at the museum?

That's not what'll happen, Mark thought. Long before anything like that goes on, Joe is going to notice that my headphones aren't connected to anything.

The pretense of being on the tour was only meant to fool casual observers. Mark had never considered the possibility that someone might latch onto him.

If Joe finds out I've got no tape player . . .

No telling what he might do. For starters, he'll probably ask a lot of questions. Then he might report me.

Mark put his hand on Joe's shoulder. Joe shut off his player and turned his head.

Grimacing, Mark said, 'Gotta go.'

'What's up?'

'Don't know. Something I ate. Feels like the runs. Gotta go.'

'Okay, man. Later.'

Bent over slightly, Mark walked quickly out of the room. In the hall, he didn't look back.

If he comes with me, I'm screwed.

In case Joe was following him, Mark stayed hunched over on his way down the stairs. Plenty of people were on their way up, so he kept to the right. None paid him much attention. He could hear people behind him, too.

Please, not Joe.

At the bottom, he glanced back.

Five or six people were on their way down, but Joe wasn't among them.

Mark continued toward the front door. He was almost there before he caught himself, remembered that he *didn't* need to use the restroom, and changed course.

'Excuse me, are you all right?'

He turned toward the voice.

It belonged to a girl wearing the tan blouse and shorts of a Beast House guide. This wasn't the husky one he'd seen earlier. This guide was slender with light brown hair and a deep tan. Mark quickly looked away from her and mumbled, 'Bathroom.'

'The restrooms are around back. Just next to the gift shop.'

Nodding, he muttered, 'Thanks.'

Just great, he thought.

He started toward the front door.

Now I'll have to leave and come back in.

'A lot quicker if you go straight through,' the guide said.

He stopped and turned toward her. 'Huh?'

She pointed at the hallway beside the stairs. 'Take the hall, go through the kitchen and out the back door. When you leave the porch, the restrooms'll be straight ahead.'

'Am I allowed to go out that way?'

'Anybody tries to stop you, tell 'em Thompson says it's okay.'

'Okay. Thanks a lot.'

He hurried past her, past the foot of the stairs, and into the hallway. With a glance back, he saw that she wasn't following him. He was alone in the hallway. He quickened his pace and entered the kitchen.

Nobody in the kitchen, either.

My God, I don't believe it!

Believe it, he thought.

He hurried through the kitchen, but not toward the back door – toward the open pantry.

He entered it. Before he could reach the stairs, however, he heard voices from below.

Of course, he thought. Obviously, I can't be *that* lucky.

The cellar was at the *end* of the audio tour . . . the *pièce de résistance*. Nobody actually following the audio tour should be here yet, but some had obviously ignored the tape and rushed on ahead.

Damn!

Starting down the stairs, Mark reminded himself that his plans had never included the idea that he would find the cellar deserted. He'd just figured, if one thing led to another and he ended up *needing* the cellar as a last resort, that he would find other people here and he would need to play it by ear.

It's not exactly a last resort yet, he told himself.

But things happened and I'm here.

In the light from the dangling, bare bulb, Mark saw only four people in the cellar. A young man and woman were standing at the cordon, peering down at the hole in the dirt floor. Next to the woman stood a small girl, maybe four years old. The woman was holding her hand. Off to the side, a husky, bearded guy stood staring into the Kutch tunnel through the bars of the door.

The little girl didn't have headphones on. She looked over her shoulder at Mark and said, 'Hi.'

Mark smiled. 'Hi.'

The mother frowned down at the girl. 'Don't bother the man, honey.'

'It's all right,' he said.

The bearded guy turned around and said to Mark, 'A shame they don't open up the tunnel.'

'Yeah,' Mark said.

'I'd love to see the tunnel.'

'Me, too.'

'*And* the Kutch house.'

'Yeah. Same here.'

'I mean, that's where half the good stuff happened and we don't even get to see it.'

'Well, it's still occupied.'

'I know that,' the man said, seeming a bit miffed that Mark doubted the breadth of his knowledge. 'Maggie's daughter. What I hear, she's as deranged as her mother was. Five'll get you ten she's got a critter or two over there right now.'

'Maybe,' Mark said. He turned away from the man, approached the cordoned-off area around the hole in the floor, and stepped up beside the little girl. The mother and father looked at him, then returned their attention to the hole.

Mark looked at it, too, though he'd seen it many times before.

Just a hole in the dirt, probably only a couple of feet in diameter.

Can I fit in there? he wondered. Sure. I must. It's big enough for the beasts and they're bigger than me.

'That's where the beast comes out,' he explained in a voice plenty loud enough for everyone to hear.

The little girl looked up at him. Her parents turned their heads.

'We know,' said her father. 'We've seen the movies, too.'

'Have you read the books?' Mark asked.

The father shook his head and resumed looking at the hole.

'What're you looking at?' Mark asked.

'What do you think?' the father asked.

The mother gave Mark a tiny frown.

'Waiting for the beast to come out?' Mark asked.

'Please,' the man said.

'It might, you know.'

The girl, gazing up at him, raised her eyebrows.

'Yesterday,' Mark said, 'a beast came popping up out of this very hole and snatched a little girl.' He put a hand on her shoulder. 'She was just your size.'

'Don't touch my daughter,' the mother said.

'Excuse me.' He removed his hand.

The father glared at him.

'And stop trying to scare her,' the mother said.

'I'm not trying to scare her. I just wanted to warn her. This big white naked beast actually popped up yesterday and grabbed a little girl no bigger than your daughter and dragged her down into the hole with it.'

The daughter looked good and scared.

Her father whirled toward Mark. 'Look, kid . . .'

'The girl was *screaming*.'

The mother said to her daughter, 'He's making this

up, Nancy. He's a *mean* person and . . .'

Crouching low enough to look the girl straight in the eyes, Mark said, 'It *ate* her up!'

She screamed.

The mother threw her arms around the girl.

The father stomped toward Mark. Red in the face, he stormed, 'That's enough out of you, young man! That's *more* than enough!'

Putting up his open hands, Mark backed away. 'Hey, hey. Take it easy, okay? I'm just concerned about your little girl, man. You don't *want* her to get eaten up by a beast, do you?'

The girl screamed again.

'We're getting out of here,' the mother blurted. She picked up the girl. 'You, too, Fred. Come with us right now.' She hurried toward the stairway.

Fred glared at Mark, then looked at his wife and said, 'I'll be right with you, honey.'

'*Now!* He's just a trouble-maker. He probably wants you to hit him so he can sue us. Don't give him the satisfaction.'

He nodded. 'I'll be right with you.'

'No you won't. You'll come *now*!'

Fred sighed. Then he leaned in close to Mark and snarled, 'What I oughta do, you little fuck, is rip off your head and shit down your neck.'

'What you oughta do,' Mark said, 'is lay your hands on some original material.'

Fred cried out in rage and reached for Mark's neck.

As Mark lurched backward, the wife yelled, '*FRED! NO!*' and the bearded man leaped out in front of Fred to hold him back.

'It's all right, fella,' the bearded guy said. 'Take it easy, take it easy. The kid's just a little wise-ass. Don't let him get to you. Huh? Come on, now. Come on.'

Holding Fred like a friend, the bearded guy walked him toward the stairway.

With the sobbing child in her arms, the mother climbed the stairs backward to keep her eyes on the situation.

Fred, still held by the bearded guy, started up the stairs. He muttered, 'It's okay. I'm fine. You can let go.'

But the bearded guy held on.

Near the top of the stairs, the mother halted. In a shrill voice, she announced, 'You, young man, should be ashamed of yourself. You're a nasty, horrible creature. What's the *matter* with you, saying such awful things to an innocent little child! I hope your skin falls off and you rot in hell forever! And rest assured, we *will* report you! You'll be out of here on your insolent little ass!'

They resumed their climb up the stairs.

The moment all four were out of sight, Mark swung a leg over the cordon. He hurried over to the hole, sank to his knees, then leaned forward and lowered himself headfirst into the darkness.

Chapter Nine

I did it! I did it!

Feeling gleeful and scared, Mark skidded and scurried downward. The slope beneath him was very steep at first. After it leveled out, he belly-crawled forward a little farther. Then he stopped and lowered his head against his arms.

He was breathing hard. His heart was thudding. Though he felt sweaty all over, the air in the tunnel was cool. It smelled of moist earth, but the dirt beneath him didn't seem wet.

I can't believe I made it, he thought.

I can't believe I *did* that!

Damn! he thought. Hope I didn't warp the little girl for life.

He laughed, but kept it quiet so the quick bursts of air only came out his nostrils and he sounded like a sniffing dog.

Stop it, he told himself.

For a while, he heard nothing except his own

heartbeat and quiet breathing. Then came faint voices. A man's voice. A woman's. He couldn't hear them well, or what was being said, but he imagined the little girl's father was in the cellar with one of the female guides – maybe the pretty one, Thompson, who had given Mark directions to the restroom.

The bastard was right here.

Well, he doesn't seem to be here now.

He imagined the two of them roaming through the cellar, looking behind the various crates and steamer trunks scattered about the floor.

Maybe he went down in the hole.

That's not very likely, sir. What he probably did was hurry upstairs as soon as you left.

I happen to think he's hiding in the hole. Would you please check?

Then Mark heard a voice clearly. It did sound like Thompson. 'All I can say is we'll keep an eye out for him and toss him out on his ear if we run into him. Let me know, though, if *you* see him again.'

'You can count on that, young lady.' Fred, all right.

'But I imagine he probably took off after his little stunt.'

'He *terrified* my little Nancy.'

'I understand. I'm sorry.'

'I don't know what kind of outfit you people are running here, letting a thing like that happen.'

'Well, we have a lot of visitors. Once in a while, someone gets out of hand. We do apologize. And we'll be more than happy to refund . . .' Her voice began to fade.

Mark pictured them walking away, heading for the cellar stairs. He still heard Thompson and the man, but couldn't make out their words. Then their voices were gone.

I've really made it now, Mark thought. I'm home free.

He felt sorry about causing trouble for Thompson. She seemed nice, and it was his fault she had to deal with the girl's father.

Hell, he thought, she probably has to contend with crappy people all the time. It's part of her job.

What if she comes back?

She won't, he told himself.

Maybe she suspects, just didn't want to mention it in front of Fred.

He imagined her coming back without the angry father. But with a flashlight. And maybe with a pair of coveralls to put on to keep her uniform from getting dirty.

She has temporarily closed off the cellar to tourists.

Standing just outside the cordon, she takes off her tan blouse and shorts. This surprises Mark somewhat, even thought it's only happening in his own mind. He thinks

61

maybe she is removing her uniform so it won't get sweaty when she crawls through the hole.

Apparently, she doesn't want her bra or panties to get sweaty, either. Mark can hardly blame her; who would want to spend the rest of the day wearing damp underclothes?

Now she is naked except for her shoes and socks. Balancing on one foot, she steps into her bright orange coveralls.

No longer comfortable lying flat on his belly, Mark pushed with his knee and rolled a little so most of his weight was on his right side.

Why bother wearing the jumpsuit? he thought. Why not just crawl in naked? She can hose herself off afterward.

For a few moments, Mark was able to picture her coming through the tunnel naked on her elbows and knees, her wobbling breasts almost touching the dirt.

She wouldn't do it naked, he thought. She's coming in after *me*, so she'll be wearing the jumpsuit.

But *just* the jumpsuit.

Its top doesn't have to be zipped all the way up. It can be like halfway down, or maybe all the way to her belly button, and . . .

'This is it?' asked a woman's voice.

'This is it.' A man.

'It's just a hole.'

'It's hardly *just* a hole. It's the *beast* hole. It's how the beast came into the house.'

'I'm sure.'

'Well, I think you'd feel differently if you'd read the books.'

'I saw the movies.'

'It's not the same. I mean . . . this is the *beast* hole.'

'And quite a hole it is.'

'Jeez, Helen.'

'Sorry.'

They went silent.

A little while later, a male voice said, 'I suppose it's all quite Freudian, actually.'

Someone giggled.

'Am I being naughty?' the same man asked.

'Shhhh.'

More voices.

Voices came and went.

As time passed, it seemed ever less likely that Thompson or anyone else would be coming into the hole to search for Mark.

This is so great, he thought. I've really made it. Now all I have to do is wait here until the place closes.

He imagined himself opening the back door at midnight, Alison's surprise – *My God, you really did it!* – and she steps into the house and puts her arms around him, kisses him.

'HELLLLLLL-OOOOOHHHHH!!!'

He flinched.

'HELL-OOOHHHH DOWN DARE, LITTLE BEASTIE BEASTIE!'

Apparently, just a zany tourist.

As time passed, he found that yelling into the hole was a favorite pastime of people visiting the cellar.

Every so often, a loud voice came down to startle him.

'Yoo-hooo! Any beasts down there?'

'Hey! Come on up! Ellen wants to check out the equipment!'

'*Guten Morgen, Herr Beast! Was gibt?*'

'Hey! Come on up and say hi!'

At one point, a woman yelled, 'Yo, down there! I'm ready if yer willin'!'

A while later, a man called, '*Bon jour, Monsieur bete!*'

He heard languages that made no sense to him. Some sounded Oriental, some Slavic. Some people who called into the hole spoke the English language with accents suggesting they came from the deep south, the northeast, Ireland, France, England, Italy, Australia. One sounded like the Frances McDormand character in *Fargo*.

Men shouted into the hole. So did women. So did quite a few children.

When women shouted, their husbands or boyfriends seemed to enjoy it.

When guys shouted, their female companions sometimes laughed but more often told them, 'Stop that' or 'Don't be so childish.'

When children shouted, some mothers seemed to find it cute but others scolded. 'Hush!' And, 'What do you think you're doing?' And, 'Quit that!' Sometimes, immediately after shouting a cheerful, *'Hiya, beast!'* or *'Betcha can't catch me!'* into the hole, kids cried out, *'OW!'* Some squealed. Others began to cry.

A couple of times, Mark heard mothers warn their kids, 'The monster'll come out and get you, if you don't behave.'

Mark listened to it all, sometimes smiling, sometimes angry, often grinning as he imagined himself springing up out of the hole at them.

Oh, how they would scream and run!

Except for the shouts, most of the voices weren't very loud. Some, so soft that Mark couldn't make out the words, formed a soothing murmur. He found himself drowsing off. It hardly surprised him, considering that he'd spent most of last night lying awake.

He fell asleep without realizing it, listening to the voices, his mind often wandering through memories and fantasies but eventually taking a subtle turn into dreams that seemed very real and sometimes wonderful and sometimes horrid. Then a shout would startle him awake. Sometimes, he woke up frightened, grateful to the shouter. Other times, the shout came just in time to prevent Alison or Officer Chaney or Thompson from coming naked into his arms and he woke up aroused and wanted to kill the shouter.

He never knew quite how long he'd been asleep.

Though he wore a wristwatch, he tried to avoid checking it. The more often you check the time, he thought, the more slowly it goes by.

So he waited and waited.

At last, figuring that it must be at least three o'clock in the afternoon, he raised his head and pushed the button on the side of his watch. The numbers lit up.

12:35.

He groaned.

'*I heard it!*' a kid yelled. '*I heard the beast!*'

Chapter Ten

'You didn't hear shit,' said someone else. The kid's sister?

'Watch your tongue, young lady.' Her father?

'I heard it, Dad! I heard it groan! It's the beast! It's in the hole!'

'There's no such thing as beasts, dipshit.'

'Julie!'

'So sorry.'

The boy said, 'It made a noise like, *uhnnnn.*'

'Oh, sure.'

'You just didn't hear it 'cause of your earphones.'

A moment later, the father said, 'It doesn't appear that anyone else heard this groan of yours, either.'

'It's not *my* groan, it's the *beast's*! And they've *all* got earphones on! Everybody's got earphones on! There's a *beast* in the hole! We gotta *tell* somebody!'

'Is there a problem?' asked a new voice. It sounded like a middle-aged woman.

'I heard a beast in the hole!'

'Really? What did it say?'

'Didn't say nothing.'

'Anything,' the father said.

'It went, *grrrrrrr.*'

Now the kid's going weird, Mark thought.

'Edith?' Another new voice. A man.

'This young fellow says he heard a growl coming from the hole.'

'Haven't heard anything like that, myself.'

'You had your earphones on,' the boy argued.

'I'm afraid my son has a very active imagination,' his father said. 'At home, he has a monster under his bed and another one in his closet and . . .'

'Don't forget the green monster in the basement,' the sister chimed in.

Thank you thank you thank you, Mark thought.

'But I *heard* it. It came from the hole.'

'*You're* the hole.'

'Julie!'

'Just kidding.'

'Come on, kids. We're disturbing everyone. Let's go.'

'But *Daaaaad.*'

'You heard me.'

'Don't be too hard on the boy,' said the voice of Edith's husband. 'An imagination's a good thing to have.'

'But I didn't . . .'

'*Ralph!*'

'Okay, okay. I didn't hear nothing.'

'Anything.'

'Dip.'

'Julie.'

'Have a nice day, folks,' said Edith.

'Thank you.' The father's voice faded as he said, 'Sorry about the disturbance.'

That was a close one, Mark thought.

Then he thought worse.

What if Ralph tells Thompson what he heard? Instead of passing it off as a figment of the kid's imagination, she might put two and two together.

They've probably browbeaten the kid into silence, Mark thought.

The chances of Thompson hearing about the groan were slim to none.

But he waited, listening, so tense he could hardly breathe, ready to scurry deeper into the tunnel at the first sound of trouble.

If it's going to happen, he thought, it'll happen soon. In the next five or ten minutes.

He looked at his wristwatch.

12:41.

Only six minutes since my groan!

He lowered his face onto his crossed arms, took a deep breath and almost sighed. But he stopped the sigh and eased his breath out quietly.

It'll be all right, he told himself. Nobody's going to come down here looking for me . . . unless I make more noise!

Sounds sure do carry through here.

He wished he'd gone farther into the tunnel before stopping. Too late, now. He didn't dare to move.

Only twelve forty-one. Maybe forty-two by now.

Five hours to go before the house closes.

Five hours and fifteen minutes.

Time enough to watch five episodes of *The X Files*. Ten episodes of *The Simpsons*. You could read a whole book if it wasn't too long.

Five hours. *More* than five hours.

Almost one o'clock, now . . .

I haven't eaten all day!

He suddenly thought about the two ham-and-cheese sandwiches in his pack. A can of Pepsi in there, too. He felt the weight of them against his back, just above his buttocks. He could get to them easily, but there would be noise when he unzipped the pack . . . more noise when he unwrapped a sandwich . . . and how about the *PUFFT!* that would come if he should pop open the tab of his Pepsi?

Can't risk it, he thought.

I'll have to wait. After six, I can have a feast.

Soon, his stomach growled.

Oh my God, no!

No comments came.

His stomach rumbled.

Maybe no one's there right now, he thought. Or they're all listening to the audio tour.

People with headphones on, whether listening to music or talk radio or the Beast House tape, always seemed to be off in their own little worlds.

'*Monstruo!*'

Jeez!

'*Buenas dias, Monstruo!*'

That's enough, he thought. He lifted his head, stared for a few moments into the total blackness, then began squirming forward, deeper into the tunnel. He moved very slowly and carefully. Except for his heartbeats and breathing, he heard only the soft whisper of his windbreaker and jeans rubbing the dirt.

As the guy topside yelled what sounded like, '*No hay cabras en la piscina!*', Mark realized the voice was giving him cover noise. He suddenly picked up speed.

'Don't you saaaay that,' protested a female voice. 'He think you loco, come up 'n bite you face off.'

'He fuckin' try, I kill his ass.'

'You so tough.'

As the male grumbled something, Mark halted and lowered his head. He had no idea how much farther into the tunnel he'd squirmed. Another six feet? Maybe more like ten or fifteen.

No way to tell, but the voices from up top were muffled and less distinct than before.

Time to eat!

He rolled onto his side, unfastened the plastic buckle of his pack belt, and swung the pack into the darkness in front of him. Propped up on his elbows, he found the zipper. He pulled it slowly, quietly.

The voices far behind him were barely audible.

How about some light on the subject?

He took out a candle and a book of matches.

Lunch by candlelight.

He would need both hands for striking a match, so he set the candle down. Then he flipped open the matchbook and tore out one of the matches. He shut the cover. By touch, he found the friction surface. Then he turned his face aside, shut his eyes and struck the match.

Its flare looked bright orange through his eyelids.

An instant later, the flame settled down and he opened his eyes.

The tunnel, a tube of gray clay, was slightly wider than his shoulders but higher than he'd imagined. High enough to allow crawling on hands and knees.

In front of him, the yellowish glow from his candle lit a few more feet of tunnel before fading into the darkness.

He picked up his candle. Holding it in one hand, he

tried to light its wick as the match's flame crept toward his thumb and finger. Just when the heat began to hurt, the wick caught fire. He shook out the match.

The candle seemed brighter than the match had been.

Bracing himself up on his right elbow, he reached forward and tried to stand it upright on the tunnel floor. He tried here and there. Each time, the ground was hard and uneven and the candle wouldn't stay up by itself.

He reached out farther and tried another place. Just under the dirt, something wobbled.

A rock, maybe.

If he could get it out, the depression might make a good holder for the candle.

He worked at it.

The object came up fairly easily.

Someone's eyeglasses.

Chapter Eleven

Mark planted the candle upright at one end of the slight depression the glasses had left behind. When he let go, the candle remained standing. It was wobbly, though. He packed some dirt around its base and that helped.

Then he picked up the unearthed glasses. Braced up on both elbows, he held them with one hand and brushed them off with the other.

The upsweep of the tortoise-shell frame made him suppose the glasses had belonged to a woman. The lens on the left was gone, but the other lens seemed to be intact. It was clear glass, untinted.

Except for the missing lens, the spectacles seemed to be intact. Mark unfolded the earpieces. Their hinges worked fine. He looked more closely. Dirty, but not rusty.

How long had the glasses been down here? A few days? A month or two? A year?

How the hell did they *get* here?

All sorts of possibilities, he thought. Maybe a gal was hiding down here the same as me.

But why did she leave her glasses behind?

Easy. Because they got broken.

No. If you lose a lens, you don't throw away the whole pair of glasses. You keep them and get the lens replaced.

She might've *lost* them.

What, they fell off her face?

Fell off her face, all right. *While she was being dragged through the tunnel . . .*

Mark's stomach let out a long, grumbling growl.

He set the glasses down, reached into his pack and removed a ham-and-cheese sandwich. He opened one side of the cellophane wrapper. As he ate the sandwich, he peeled away more of the cellophane, keeping it between his filthy hands and the bread.

He decided not to bother with his Pepsi. It would've been too much trouble. Besides, his sandwich was good and moist.

As he ate, he wondered what to do with the glasses. Leave them where he'd found them? He couldn't see any purpose in that. He might as well keep them.

And do what? Take them to the police?

You found them where, young man?

In the beast tunnel.

In the WHAT?

Yeah sure, he thought. Thanks, but no thanks.

But they might be evidence of a crime.

Might not be.

What if I show them to Officer Chaney?

Show them to her in private, like 'off the record', and we can work on the case together?

He imagined himself coming down into the cellar late at night with Officer Chaney to show her where he'd found the glasses.

They both have flashlights. At the edge of the hole, she hands him a jumpsuit. She has another for herself. *Don't want to get our clothes dirty*, she explains. Then she starts to remove her police uniform.

Like *that'll* happen, Mark thought.

What'll really happen, I'll end up getting reamed for being down here in the first place.

I can at least show the glasses to Alison, he decided. She'll probably think they're pretty interesting and mysterious.

Done eating, Mark used the cellophane to wrap the glasses.

He put them into his pack.

Then he reached out, pulled the candle from its loose bed in the dirt, and puffed out its flame. A tiny orange dot remained in the darkness. Slowly, the dot faded out. He waited a while longer, then found the wick with his thumb and forefinger. It was a little warm. Squeezing it, he felt the charred part crumble.

He returned the candle and match book to his pack, then zippered the pack shut, slid it out of the way, and settled down to continue his wait.

Though he tried to relax, his mind lingered on the glasses.

There hadn't been a beast attack in years. The last two situations had taken place all the way back in 1978 and 1979. In Janice Crogan's books, *The Horror at Malcasa Point* and *Savage Times*, Mark had seen photos of all the women involved: Donna Hayes and her daughter, Sandy; Tyler Moran; Nora Branson; Janice herself, and Agnes and Maggie Kutch, of course. From what he could recall of the photos, he was almost certain that none of the women wore glasses. Maybe *sun*glasses. One snapshot had shown Sandy Hayes, Donna's twelve-year-old daughter, in sunglasses and a swimsuit.

She disappeared!

She was never seen again after the slaughter of '79.

Had she been wearing *prescription* sunglasses in the photo? Could these be her *regular* glasses? Had she been dragged away by a surviving beast and lost them here in the tunnel? Or maybe lost them while escaping through here?

Difficult to picture a cute little blonde like Sandy – who'd looked a lot like Jodie Foster at that age –

wearing such a hideous pair of tortoise-shell eyeglasses.

Besides, she'd vanished almost twenty years ago. These glasses *couldn't* have been in the dirt of the tunnel for that long.

If they're not Sandy's . . .

They could've ended up in the tunnel in all sorts of ways, Mark told himself. But they obviously suggested that a woman had been down here not terribly long ago. And that she hadn't been able to retrieve them after they fell – or were knocked – off her face. Meaning she was probably a victim of foul play.

Someone must've dragged her through this very tunnel.

Someone, something.

A beast?

They're all dead, he reminded himself. They were killed off in '79.

Says who?

Chapter Twelve

Mark lifted his head off his arms and gazed into the blackness.

What if they're wrong? he thought. What if one of the beasts survived and it's *in here* with me? Just up ahead. Maybe it knows I'm here and it's just waiting for the right moment to come and get me?

Quit it, he told himself. There isn't a beast in here.

Besides, even if there is, the things are nocturnal. They sleep all day.

Says who?

The books. The movies.

That doesn't make it true.

Into the darkness, he murmured, 'Shit.'

And he almost expected an answer.

None came, but the fear of it raised gooseflesh all over his body.

I've gotta get out of here.

Can't. I can't leave now. Not after all this. Just a few more hours . . .

In his fear, however, he decided to turn himself around. No harm in that. He would need to do it anyway, sooner or later, unless he intended to crawl all the way back to the cellar feet-first.

He took hold of his pack.

Is everything in it?

He thought so, but he didn't want to leave anything behind.

Just a quick look.

He unzipped his pack and found the matchbook. Opened it. Plucked out a match. Pressed its head against the friction surface.

Then thought about how it would light him up.

And saw himself as if through a pair of eyes deeper in the tunnel . . . eyes that hadn't seen him before . . . belonging to a man or beast who hadn't known he was here. But knows *now*.

Don't be a wuss, he told himself. Nobody's down here but me.

Who says?

Anyway, I've got everything. I don't have to light any match to know that.

We don't need no steenkin' matches!

He lowered the zipper of his windbreaker, then slipped the matchbook and the unlit match into his shirt pocket.

Now?

He shut the pack, pulled it in against his chest and began struggling to reverse his direction. The walls of the tunnel were so close to his sides that he couldn't simply turn around. He didn't even try. Instead, he got to his knees in hopes of rolling backward.

The tunnel ceiling seemed too low. The back of his head pushed at it. His neck hurt. His chin dug into his chest.

As he fought to bring his legs forward, he almost panicked with the thought that he might become stuck. Then he forced one leg out from under him. Then the other. Both legs forward, he dropped a few inches. His rump met the tunnel floor and the pressure went away from his head and neck and he flopped onto his back. He lay there gasping.

Did it!

Would've been a lot easier, he supposed, just to crawl backward. But he'd succeeded. It was over now.

What if I'd gotten stuck?

Didn't happen. Don't think about it.

He still needed to roll over, but he didn't feel like doing it just yet. Lying on his back felt good.

If I'd brought my Walkman, he thought, I could listen to some music and . . .

My headphones!

He touched his head, his neck.

The headphones were gone, all right. The loss gave him a squirmy feeling.

Where are they?

He knew for sure that he'd been wearing them when he ran into Thompson near the front door. And he'd kept them on when he went down into the cellar. And when he'd said that stuff to the little girl. But what about after her father went after him?

He didn't know.

He tried to remember if he'd still been wearing the headphones when he dived into the hole.

No idea.

He sure hoped so. If he'd lost them in the tunnel, no big deal; he would probably find them on the way out. But finding them wasn't his main concern.

If they'd fallen off his head *before* the tunnel, then someone might find them in the cellar and put two and two together.

Someone like Thompson.

But she'd already been down in the cellar looking for him. If the headphones had been there, she – or that girl's asshole of a father, Fred – probably would've found them.

I lost them down here, Mark told himself. It's all right. They're here in the tunnel somewhere.

With the small pack resting on his chest, he raised his arms and put his folded hands underneath his head.

His elbows touched the walls of the tunnel.

I'll probably find them on my way out, he thought. And if I don't, no big deal.

Someone coming into the tunnel next month . . . or next year . . . or twenty years from now might find them and wonder how they got here and wonder if they'd fallen off the head of a victim of the beast.

Little will they know.

The truth can be a very tricky thing, he thought.

A voice, muffled by distance, called, '*Heeeerre beastie-beastie-beastie!*'

Dumb ass, Mark thought.

'*Heeerre, beastie! Got something for you!*'

He imagined himself letting out a very loud, ferocious growl. It almost made him laugh, but he held it in.

A while later, he thought about looking at his wristwatch.

But he felt too comfortable to move.

Why bother anyway? It's still *way* too early to leave. It'll be hours and hours.

Hours to go . . .

A couple of years ago, Mark had memorized Frost's poem, 'Stopping by the Woods on a Snowy Evening'. Now, to pass the time, he recited it in his mind.

He also knew Kipling's 'Danny Deever', by heart, so he went through that one.

Then he tried 'The Cremation of Sam McGee', but he'd only memorized about half of it.

After that, he started on Poe's 'The Raven'. Somewhere along the way, he got confused and repeated a stanza and then it all seemed to scatter apart . . . *dreaming dreams no mortal ever dared to scheme before . . . scheming dreams . . . dreaming screams upon the bust of Alice . . . still is screaming, still is screaming . . .*

It *had* been a raven. He thought for sure it had been a raven at first, but not anymore. It was still a very large bird, but now it had skin instead of feathers. Dead white, slimy skin and white eyes that made him think it might be blind.

Blind from spending too much time in black places underground.

But if it's blind, how come I can't lose it?

It kept after Mark, no matter what he did. He felt as if it had been after him for hours.

It'll keep after me till it gets me!

Gonna get me like the birds got Suzanne Pleshette.

Peck out my eyes.

Oh, God!

Mark was now running across a field of snow. A flat, empty field without so much as a tree to hide behind. Under the full moon, the snow seemed almost to be lighted from within.

No place to hide.

The awful bird flapped close behind him. He didn't dare look back.

Suddenly, a stairway appeared in front of him. A wooden stairway, leading upward. He couldn't see what might be at the top.

Maybe a door?

If there's a door and I can get through it in time, I can shut the bird out!

He raced up the stairs.

No door at the top.

A gallows.

A hanging body.

Gus Goucher?

Maybe not. Gus belonged on the Beast House porch, not out here . . . wherever out here might be. And Gus always wore his jeans and plaid shirt, but this man was naked.

Naked and dangling in front of Mark, his bare feet just above the floor and only empty night behind him . . . empty night and a long fall . . . a fall that looked endless.

Mark had no choice.

He slammed into the man's body, hugged him around the waist and held on for dear life as they both swung out over the abyss. The rope creaked.

What if it breaks?

'Gotcha now,' the man said.

The voice sounded familiar. Mark looked up. The face of the hanged man was tilted downward, masked by shadow.

'Who are you?' Mark blurted. 'What do you want?'

'First, I'm gonna rip off your head.'

Fred!

Though they were now far out over the abyss, Mark let go. He began to drop – then stopped, his head clamped tight between Fred's hands.

'You aren't going anyplace, young man. Not till I'm done with you.'

With a sudden wrench, the hanged man jerked Mark's head around.

Mark stared out behind himself, knowing his head was backward, his neck was broken.

Oh God, no. I'm killed.

Or maybe I'll live, but I'll be totally wrecked for life, a miserable cripple like Bigelow.

And out in the moonlit night not very far in front of his eyes flapped the dead white, skin-covered bird.

'Get out of here!' Mark yelled at it. 'Leave me alone!'

'Nevermore, asshole.'

A moment later, Mark's neck gave way.

Fred's bare legs caught his torso and kept it.

Apparently, he had no more use for Mark's head.

Falling, Mark gazed up at the swinging naked man and at his own headless body.

Oh my God, he's really going to do it! And I'll get to watch! I don't want to see him do THAT to me!

Then Mark saw the fleshy white bird swoop down at him and realized it meant to grant his wish.

'*Yah!*' he cried out, and lurched awake in total darkness.

He was gasping, drenched with sweat, still sick with terror and revulsion.

Jeez!

For a moment, he thought he must be home in bed in the middle of the night. But this was no mattress under him.

Oh, yeah.

Better stay awake a little while, he told himself.

He'd heard you can get the same nightmare back if you return to sleep too quickly.

Not much danger of that, he thought.

For one thing, he felt wide awake. For another, he needed to urinate.

Man, I don't wanta do that in here.

Might have to, he thought. I can't leave here till after six, and it's probably . . . what? . . . three or three-thirty?

He brought his hands over his face, pushed the cuff of his windbreaker up his left arm and pressed a button on the side of his wristwatch.

The digital numbers lit up bright red.

6:49.

Chapter Thirteen

He'd actually slept *past* the Beast House closing time!

Fan*tas*tic!

He turned himself over. Holding the belly pack by its belt, he started squirming forward through the darkness. Soon, the fingers of his right hand snagged a thin cord.

All right!

He pulled at the cord and retrieved his headphones.

Holding the headphones in one hand, his pack in the other, he continued to squirm forward. He stopped when he came to a steep upward slope . . . the slope he'd skidded down head-first when he plunged into the hole.

Almost out.

No light came down into the tunnel. No sound, either.

The whole house should be locked up by now, everybody gone for the night.

Everybody but me!

He grinned, but he felt trembly inside.

This is *so* cool, he thought.

Then he realized that his mother and father should both be home by now. Had they found his note yet? Probably.

They're probably both mad as hell, he thought.

And worried sick.

He felt a little sick, himself.

I had to do it, he thought. How else was I going to get a date with Alison?

In his mother's voice, he heard, *Maybe you should think twice about WANTING to date a girl who would ask you to do something like this.*

'Yeah, sure,' he muttered, and scurried up the steep slope. Not stopping at the top, he crawled over the edge of the hole and across the dirt floor of the cellar until his shoulder bumped into a stanchion. The post wobbled, making clinky sounds.

Mark went around it, then stood up. It felt good to be on his feet. He fastened his belly pack around his waist, put his headphones inside it, then closed the pack. Hands free, he stretched and sighed.

I've really made it! I've got the whole place to myself!

And about five hours to kill.

First thing I'd better do, he thought, is take a leak.

But the public restrooms were outside. Now that he was in, he had no intention of leaving, not even for a few minutes.

If the house had an inside toilet, it wasn't on the audio tour and he had no idea where it might be.

Might not even be hooked up.

Well, the cellar had a dirt floor.

What if I bring Alison down here?

He imagined her pointing at a patch of wetness in the dirt. *What's that?*

Oh, I had to take a leak.

And you did it right here on the floor? That's disgusting. What, were you raised in a barn?

No, she wouldn't say anything like that. Would she?

How about doing it in the hole?

No, no. What if Alison wants to see where I found the glasses?

Hey, Mark, it's sorta muddy down here.

He chuckled.

She wouldn't *really* want to go in the hole, would she?

Who knows? She might. I'd better not piss in it.

Maybe over in a corner, behind some crates and things.

He took a candle out of his pack, removed the matches from his shirt pocket and lit it. The candle's glow spread out from the flame like a golden mist, illuminating himself, the nearby air, the dirt of the cellar floor, the brass stanchion and red plush cordon, and the hole a few feet beyond the cordon. Just beyond the hole, the glow faded out and all he could see was the dark.

Do I really want to go over there?

Not very much.

Even while in the cellar for tours during the day, he had never gone roaming through the clutter beyond the hole. Partly, he'd been afraid it might be off limits and a guide might yell at him. Partly, though, he'd always felt a little uneasy about what might be over there . . . maybe crouching among the stacked crates and trunks.

He certainly didn't want to venture into that area now, alone in the dark.

Especially since there was no real *need* for it.

Pick somewhere else, he told himself. Somewhere *close*.

He turned around slowly. Just where the glow from his candle began to fade, he saw the bottom of the stairway. He continued to turn. Straight ahead, but beyond the reach of his candle light, was the barred door to the Kutch tunnel. Though he couldn't see it, he knew it had to be there.

An idea struck him.

He chuckled softly.

Awesome.

He walked forward and the door came into sight. So did the opening behind its vertical iron bars. From the tours, books and movies, he knew that the underground passageway led westward, went under Front Street and ended in the cellar of the Kutch house.

Agnes Kutch still lived there. The locked door was meant to protect her from tourists.

And maybe to protect tourists from Agnes . . . and whatever else might be in her house. Even though all the beasts were supposed to be dead . . .

You never know.

And so with a certain relish and a little fear, Mark walked up to the door. Level with his chin was a flat, steel crossbar. He dripped some wax on it, then stood the candle upright.

Both hands free, he lowered the zipper of his jeans. He freed his penis, made sure he was between bars, then aimed high and let fly.

When Alison sees *this*, he thought, she'll never suspect it was me.

I ought to make *sure* she sees it.

Oh, my God! she might say. *Look at that! Somebody . . . went to the bathroom there!*

Somebody, Mark would say. *Or someTHING. Maybe the rumors are true.*

And she says, *Thank God this gate is locked.*

When she says that, maybe I'll put my arm around her and say, *Don't worry, Alison. I won't let anything happen to you.*

After he says that, she turns to him and puts her arms around him and he feels the pressure of her body.

Imagining it, he began to stiffen. By the time he was

95

done urinating, he had a full erection. He shook it off, then had to bend over a little and push to get it back inside his jeans and underwear.

After zipping up, he pulled at the candle. Glued in place with dried wax, it held firm for a moment before coming off . . . and Mark felt the door swing toward him.

His heart gave a rough lurch.

He took hold of an upright bar, gently pulled, and felt the door swing closer to him.

Chapter Fourteen

Mark groaned.

He eased the gate shut, leaned his forehead against a couple of the bars and looked down between them. The lock hasp on the other side was open. The padlock, always there in the past, was gone.

Oh, boy.

In his mind, he whirled around and raced up the cellar stairs and ran through the house. He made it out safely and shut the front door behind him.

In the next version of his escape, he got halfway up the cellar stairs before a beast leaped on his back and dragged him down.

Take it easy, he told himself. If one of those things *is* down here, it hasn't done anything yet. Maybe it isn't interested in nailing me. Maybe it *wants* me to leave.

Hell, there isn't any beast down here. Who ever heard of an animal taking a *padlock* off a door?

Maybe Agnes Kutch took it off.

Someone sure did, that was for certain.

I could go through and take a peek at the Kutch house.

No way, he thought. No way, no way.

Leaving the gate shut, he slowly backed away. Then he turned toward the stairs.

Just take it easy, he told himself. Pretend nothing's wrong. Whistle a happy tune.

Man, I'm *not* gonna whistle.

On his way to the stairs, he listened. His own shoes made soft brushing sounds against the hard dirt floor. No sounds came from behind him. No growls. No huffing breath. No rushing footfalls. Nothing.

He put his foot on the first stair and started up. The wooden plank creaked.

Please please please.

Second stair.

Just let me get out of here. Please.

Third.

No sound except a squeak of wood under his weight.

He wanted to rush up the rest of the stairs, but feared that such sudden quick movements might bring on an attack.

He climbed another stair, another.

So far, so good.

Now he was high enough for the glow of his candle to reach the uppermost stair.

Almost there.

I'll never make it.

Please let me make it! I'm sorry I scared the girl. I'm sorry I pissed through the bars.

He climbed another stair and imagined a beast down in the cellar suddenly springing out from behind some crates and coming for him.

Silently.

I'm sorry! Please! Don't let it get me! Let me get out of here and I'll go home and never pull another dumbass stunt in my life.

Almost to the top. And maybe the beast was almost upon him even though he couldn't hear it and didn't dare look back, so he took the next step slowly. And the next. And then he was in the pantry.

Go!

He broke into a run. The gust of quick air snuffed his candle.

Shit!

But the way ahead had a gray hint of light and he ran toward it. Suddenly in the kitchen, he skidded to a halt and whirled around and found the pantry door and swung it shut.

It slammed.

Mark cringed.

He leaned back against the door. Heart thudding hard and fast, he huffed for air.

Made it! I made it! Thank you thank you thank you!

But he suddenly imagined being hurled across the kitchen as the beast crashed through the door.

Gotta get outa here!

He lurched forward, turned and hurried through the kitchen. By the vague light coming in through its windows, he made his way to the back door. He twisted its knob and pulled, but the door wouldn't budge.

Come on!

He found its latch.

The door swung open. He rushed out onto the back porch.

About to pull the door shut, he stopped.

What if I get locked out?

Doesn't matter! I'm going home!

He let go of the door. Leaving it ajar, he backed away from it. He watched it closely.

The porch, enclosed by screens, was gray with moonlight, black with shadows. It smelled slightly of stale cigarette smoke. It had some furniture along the sides: a couch, a couple of chairs and small tables. In the corner near the kitchen was something that looked like a refrigerator.

Mark backed up until he came to a screen door. He nudged it, but it stayed shut. Turning sideways, he felt along its frame. It was secured by a hook and eye. He flicked the hook up. Then he pushed at the screen door and it swung open, squawking on its hinges.

Holding the door open, he stared out at the moonlit back lawn, the gift shop, the restrooms, the patio with the chairs upside-down on the table tops, and the snack stand. All brightly lit by the full moon. Some places dirty white, others darker. A dozen different shades of gray, it seemed. And some places that were black.

I made it, he thought.

He stepped outside and stood at the top of the porch stairs.

Safe!

Done with the candle, he opened his pack. As he put it inside, he felt the hardness of his Pepsi can. And the softness of his second sandwich. So he trotted down the stairs and walked over to the patio. He hoisted a chair off the top of a table, turned it right-side up, and set it down.

Standing next to the table, he put his hand inside his pack, intending to take out the sandwich. He felt cellophane, realized his fingers were on the eye-glasses, and pulled them out. He set them on the table, then reached into his pack again and removed the sandwich. Then the Pepsi. He put them on the table and sat down.

With his back toward Beast House.

He didn't like that, so he stood up and moved his chair. When he sat down this time, he was facing the house's back porch.

That's better, he thought.

Not that it really matters. I never would've made it out if there'd been a beast in there.

What about the padlock?

Who knows?

Somebody had obviously removed it. Earlier, the bearded guy had been standing at the gate, complaining about not being allowed to go through the tunnel to explore the Kutch house. The padlock must've been on it then.

Maybe not.

Anyway, I'm outa there.

He picked up his Pepsi, opened the plastic bag and pulled out the can. It felt moist, slightly cool. He snapped open the tab and took a drink.

Wonderful!

He set it down, peeled the cellophane away from one side of his sandwich, and took a bite.

The sandwich tasted delicious. He ate it slowly, taking a sip of Pepsi after every bite or two.

No hurry, he told himself. No hurry at all.

I'm already screwed.

If he hadn't left the note for his parents, he could walk in the door half an hour from now and be fine. Make up a story about getting delayed somewhere. Apologize like crazy. No major problem.

But he *had* left the note and they'd almost certainly found it by now.

I'll be back in the morning.

I'm *so* screwed, he thought.

We've always trusted you, Mark.

Where exactly did you go that was so important you felt it necessary to put your mother and I through this sort of hell?

We're so disappointed in you.

Sometimes I think you don't have the sense God gave little green apples.

Did it never occur to you that your father and I would be worried sick?

Maybe you should try thinking about someone other than yourself for a change.

He sighed.

It would be at least that bad, maybe worse. What if Mom *cries*? What if *Dad* cries?

All this grief, he thought, and for nothing . . . didn't even make it till midnight for my date with Alison.

Says who?

Chapter Fifteen

He kept his eyes on Beast House, especially on the screen door of the porch.

When he was done with his meal, he put his Pepsi can into the plastic bag. They went into his belly pack. So did his sandwich wrapper and the eyeglasses.

He turned the chair upside-down and placed it on top of the table.

Then he walked over to the men's restroom. The door was locked. No surprise there. But the area in front of the door was cloaked in deep shadows. He would be well hidden there. He sat down and leaned back against the wall.

And waited, keeping his eyes on Beast House.

Also watching the rear grounds.

Ready to leap up and run in case of trouble.

The concrete wasn't very comfortable. He often changed positions. Sometimes, his butt fell asleep. Sometimes, one leg or the other. Every once in a while, he stood up and wandered around to get his circulation going again.

When 11:30 finally arrived, he went to the other side of the gift shop. There, standing in almost the same place where he'd jumped down from the roof that morning, he began to pee in the grass. And he remembered the dead dog on the roof.

It's probably still up there.

How did it *get* up there?

He tilted back his head and looked at the upper windows of Beast House.

He could almost see the dog flying out into the night, tumbling end over end . . .

Thinking about it, he felt his penis shrink. He shook it off, tucked it in and raised the zipper of his jeans. He hurried around the corner of the building, out of the shadows and back into moonlight.

Much better.

Waiting in the wash of the moonlight, he checked his wristwatch often. At 11:50, he walked very slowly toward the back porch . . . his gaze fixed on its screen door.

Nothing's gonna leap out at me, he told himself. It hasn't done it for the past four hours and it won't do it now. There's probably nothing in the house *to* leap out at me.

His back to the porch, he sat down on the second stair from the bottom.

Okay, he thought. I'm ready when you are.

As eager as Alison had seemed on the phone, he expected her to show up early.

He turned his head, scanning the grounds, looking for her. Of course, the various buildings blocked much of his view.

He wondered if Alison planned to climb the spiked fence.

What if she tries and doesn't make it?

He could almost hear her scream as one of the spear-like tips jammed up through the crotch of her jeans.

Five, six inches of iron, right up her . . .

Stop it.

Anyway, she'll probably hop over the turnstile, same as me. If she does, she'll be coming around from the front of the house.

He looked toward the southeast corner.

Any second now.

Seconds passed, and she didn't come walking around the corner.

Minutes passed.

12:06.

Where *is* she?

What if she doesn't show up at all? Maybe she got caught. Maybe she forgot about it. Maybe the never *meant* to show up, and it was all just a trick.

No, no. She wouldn't do that. She *wants* to come.

If she doesn't make it, it's because something went wrong.

Says who?

Me, that's who. This wasn't any trick. She wouldn't do that sort of thing.

And then she came jogging around the corner of Beast House.

Someone did. A figure in dark clothes.

What if it's not Alison?

Has to be, he told himself.

The approaching jogger seemed to be about Alison's size, but not much showed. A hat covered her hair and she seemed to be wearing a loose, oversized shirt or jacket that hung halfway down her thighs. Or *his* thighs. For all Mark could really see, the jogger might not even be a girl.

He sat motionless on the porch stair, watching, ready to stand up and bolt.

The jogger raised an arm.

He waved and stood up.

Slowing to a brisk walk, she plucked off her hat. Her hair spilled out from under it, pale in the moonlight. 'Hiya, Mark.'

Alison's voice.

His throat tightened. 'Hi. You made it.'

'Oh, yeah. I wouldn't miss this.' A stride away from him, she stopped and stuffed her hat into a side pocket of her jacket. She took a few quick breaths, then shook her head. 'But I guess I wasted my time, huh?'

'I hope not.'

'You knew the rules, Mark.'

'Yeah.'

'Damn. I don't know why, but I really figured you'd be able to pull it off somehow.'

'I sorta *did*.'

Her mouth opened slightly.

'I've *been* inside.'

'Really?'

'I just . . . figured I'd meet you out here.'

'Okay. Great. Let's go in.' She started to step around him.

He put up his hand. 'No, wait.'

She halted and turned to him. 'What?'

'I'm not so sure it's safe.'

She chuckled. 'Of *course* it's not safe. Where'd be the fun in that?'

'No, I mean it. I really don't think it'd be such a great idea to go in. I think somebody might be *in* there.'

'What do you mean? Like a night-watchman? A guard?'

'I mean more like somebody who *shouldn't* be in there. Maybe even . . . you know . . . one of the *things*.'

'A *beast*? How cool would *that* be?'

'Real cool, except it might kill us.'

'Then *we* could be exhibits.' She sounded amused.

'I don't think we should go in.'

'Oh.'

'I really like you a lot and everything. It'd be fantastic to go in the house and explore around with you. I mean, God, I sure don't want to *disappoint* you. But I don't want to get you killed, either.'

In silence, she nodded a few times. Then she said, 'You didn't make it in, did you?'

'Huh?'

'You just figured you'd meet me out here anyway and hope for the best.'

'No, I got in. I did. It's open.'

'Let's go see.'

She turned away. Mark almost grabbed her, but stopped his hand in time.

She trotted up the porch stairs, opened the screen door and looked around at him. 'Well, *this* isn't locked.'

'I know.'

She went in.

Mark hurried after her. 'No, wait.'

She didn't wait. She walked straight across the porch.

'Alison. Wait up.'

She stopped and gave the kitchen door a push. It swung open. 'Hey,' she said. She sounded surprised and pleased.

'I told you.'

She turned around. 'You really *did* it. Good *going*, Mark. I had a feeling about you.'

'Well . . .'

She came toward him, stopped only inches away and put her hands on his sides. She looked into his eyes for a few seconds. When she pulled him forward, his belly pack pushed at her. 'Let's get this out of the way,' she said. She slid it around to his hip, then wrapped her arms around him and tilted back her head.

They kissed.

He had often imagined kissing Alison, and now it was happening for real. She seemed to be all smoothness and softness and warmth. She had a taste of peppermint and an outdoors aroma as if she'd taken on some of the scents of the night: the ocean breeze and the fog and the pine trees. She held him so snugly that he could feel each time she took a breath or let it out.

Though her breasts were muffled under layers of jackets and shirts, he could feel them.

He started to get hard.

Uh-oh.

Afraid it would push against her, he bent forward slightly.

Alison loosened her hold on him. 'I'm ready if you are,' she whispered.

Chapter Sixteen

'Huh?' Mark asked.

'Ready?'

Still holding each other, but loosely with their bodies barely touching, they spoke in hushed voices.

'Ready for what?'

'To go in.'

'Oh. I really don't think we should.'

'Sure we should. I've been waiting for this for *years*. It's gonna be *so* cool. Come on.' She lowered her arms, turned toward the kitchen door, then reached back and took hold of Mark's right hand. 'Come on.' She pulled at it.

He followed her into the kitchen. And stopped. 'Wait. I have to tell you something.'

She turned toward him. 'Okay.'

'I was down in the cellar. That's where I hid till closing time.'

'Really?' She sounded interested.

'Down in the beast hole.'

'My God. *Inside* it?'

'Yeah, there's like a tunnel.'

'Wow.'

'I stayed in there all day.'

'My God. How cool! Weren't you scared?'

'Sometimes.'

'So how did you return the tape player?'

'I didn't. I never got one in the first place. I came over really early and jumped the turnstile and hid until they opened the house. Then I just blended into the crowd and pretended to be a tourist till I got down into the cellar.'

'Good going.'

'I was pretty lucky. I had a couple of minutes by myself, so I crawled down the hole and stayed.'

'So *that's* how it's done.'

'How *I* did it, anyway. But the thing is, when I came out of the hole, I took a look around. You know how there's always a padlock on the Kutch side of the door down there?'

'Sure.'

'It's gone. The padlock.'

'Gone?'

'Yeah. And I'm pretty sure it was there this morning. So somebody must've taken it off while I was down in the hole.'

'The door isn't locked at all?'

'It opens. *I* opened it, just to see.'

'Did you go through?'

'The tunnel? No. I got out of there.'

'But it goes to the Kutch house.'

'I know.'

'Nobody *ever* gets to see the Kutch house. This is the chance of a lifetime.'

'Yeah, a chance to die.'

'Oh, don't be that way. Nobody's going to die.'

'That's because we're getting out of here.' Turning away, he pulled at Alison's hand.

She jerked her hand from his grip. 'Not me,' she said. 'I'm not leaving till I've checked the place out.'

'The *padlock's* off.'

'Right. Meaning we can go through the tunnel.'

'Maybe someone *already* came through. From the other side. Doesn't that *scare* you? We oughta get out of here right now. We're lucky we haven't already gotten . . .'

'Nobody's stopping you.'

'What do you mean?'

'You can go.'

'I can't leave *you* here.'

'Well, I'm not going.' She sounded so calm.

'But . . .'

'Okay, so the padlock's off. Did you get chased or anything?'

'No.'

'See anything? Hear anything?'

'No.'

'So as far as you know – except for the padlock being off – the house is as safe as ever.'

'But the padlock . . .'

'Did you actually *see* it today?'

'No, but I'm pretty sure it was there.'

'But you didn't see it with your own eyes. So maybe it *wasn't* there. When was the last time you actually *saw* it?'

'I guess maybe . . . early July.'

'I did the tour last month,' she admitted. 'I saw it then. So that's the last time we can be sure it was on the door. A month ago. So maybe it's been gone for *weeks*.'

'I don't think so. That door's *always* locked.'

'Okay. Maybe it is and maybe it isn't. But even if someone took the lock off *today*, it doesn't mean they're in the house right *now*.'

'I guess not,' he admitted.

'Come on. Let's take a look around.'

'I don't think we should. Really.'

'I do. Really.'

'Alison . . .'

'Mark. Come on. It took a lot of guts to do what you did today. You don't want to bail out now, do you?'

'Not really. But . . .'

'Then don't. Come on.' She took his hand and led him through the kitchen.

'Not the cellar,' he whispered.

'Of course, the cellar.'

'Why don't we go through the rest of the house first? Don't you want to wander around and see all the exhibits? I thought that was supposed to be the main idea.'

'It was. But this is our chance to see inside the Kutch house. Maybe our *only* chance ever.'

'I think it's a really bad idea.'

In an oddly chipper voice, Alison said, 'I don't,' and led him into the pantry.

She suddenly stopped.

'What?' Mark whispered.

'My God, it's dark in here.'

'Even darker in the cellar.'

'Do you have something?' Alison asked.

'A couple of candles.'

'Good. I meant to bring a flashlight. Glad *you* came prepared.'

'Thanks.' He let go of Alison's hand, reached over to his right hip and slid open the zipper of his pack. When he tried to put his hand in, the headphones got in his way. He took them out. 'Can you hold these?'

Alison found them in the darkness and took them.

'Thanks.'

He put his hand into the pack.

'Headphones?' Alison asked.

'To make me look like a tourist.'

'Hmm. Smarter than the av-uh-ridge bear.'

Cellophane crinkled softly.

'What's that?' she asked.

'Wrappers. I had my lunch in here. I've also got an empty Pepsi can.'

His fingertips found the match book. He took it out, opened its flap and plucked out a match. He snicked it across the score and tiny sparks leaped around the match head, but it didn't catch.

He tried again.

The match flared.

'Now we're cookin',' Alison said.

She looked golden in the glow of the small flame. Mark smiled when he saw that she was wearing the headphones.

'Why don't I hold this?' Mark suggested, 'and you reach in and get out the candles.'

'Sounds like a plan.' She slipped her fingers into the opening, then smiled at him. 'You don't have anything nasty in here, do you?'

'I don't think so.'

Her hand came out holding a pink candle. 'Here's one,' she said. She raised it and held it steady, its wick touching the flame of Mark's match.

When the candle wick caught fire, Mark shook out the match. Alison gave the candle to him.

'Thanks,' he whispered.

'I get the other one?'

'Sure. We might as well use them both.'

She put her hand into the pack again. 'What's this?'

'What's what?'

She removed her hand from the pack. And showed him.

'Somebody's glasses. I found them down in the beast hole.'

'Really? Can I have a look?'

'Sure.'

The cellophane made quiet crackly sounds as she unwrapped the glasses.

She raised them into the light of Mark's candle.

Her eyes opened very wide.

She said, 'Oh, my God.'

Chapter Seventeen

Mark suddenly felt sick. Again. 'What's wrong?' he asked.

'They're *hers*.'

'Whose?'

'Claudia's.'

'Claudia who?'

'You know, *Claudia*. I don't know her last name. That grody kid. Sorta fat and dumpy. She showed up for a while last year.'

'Oh.'

'Remember?'

'Sort of.' He vaguely recalled a pudgy girl with hair that had always looked greasy. 'She was only in school a couple of weeks, wasn't she?'

'Try three months.'

'Really?'

'I should know. She spent them all *hanging* on me.'

'Oh. She *was* always, like, following you around the halls.'

'Yeah. Like a dog. She wanted to be my friend. I hated to be *mean* to her, you know? She seemed nice enough. But *too* nice, if you know what I mean.'

'Fawning.'

'Yeah. That's it, fawning. God, she was aggravating. She would never take a hint. She never knew when to quit. She would like *invite* herself places, stuff like that. There was one time, I told her she should try to find herself some *new* friends and she said, "You're all the friend I could ever want." She was *so* awful.'

'And she disappeared?' Mark asked.

Alison stared at the glasses. Nodding, she said, 'Yeah. I mean, it wasn't like she *disappeared*. I never heard of search parties or anything. One day, she just didn't show up for school. I figured she'd stayed home because she was upset at me. I'd really laid into her the day before. Told her I was tired of having her in my face all the time and how she was driving me nuts. I was pretty rough on her. But, jeez, what're you gonna do? I mean, it was like having a stalker.'

'That was the day before she disappeared?' Mark asked.

'Yeah. And when she didn't show up for school, I was really glad about it at first. But after a couple of days, I started to feel guilty. I mean, I don't want to go around *hurting* people . . . not even her. So I finally went over to where she lived, figuring maybe to apologize. I'd been to her place once before. It was this grody trailer over in the woods . . . know where Captain Frank's old bus is?'

Mark nodded.

'Over there. So I paid a visit to her trailer and her mom said she didn't know where Claudia was. She hadn't seen her in three or four days. Figured she must've run away from home. And, "Good riddance," she said. What she really said? I couldn't believe my ears. "Good riddance to bad rubbish." Can you imagine someone saying that about her own daughter?'

'That's pretty cold,' Mark said.

'I couldn't believe it. Anyway, she seemed to think Claudia had run off to San Francisco "to live with the dykes and bums". Those are her words, not mine. "Dykes and bums". Jeez.' She turned the glasses in the candlelight. Then she muttered, 'Guess that isn't where she went.'

'They probably aren't Claudia's.'

'Oh, they're hers, all right. I mean, nobody wears glasses like these. Nobody except maybe a stand-up comic *trying* to look like a doofus. And Claudia. You'd better show me where you found them.'

'Well . . . Okay. Wanta light the other candle?'

Alison returned the glasses to Mark's pack and took out the second candle. 'Need anything else out of here?'

'I don't think so.'

She shut the zipper, then tilted her candle toward

Mark and touched her wick to his. Her wick caught fire, doubling the light.

'I'll go first,' Mark whispered, hurrying past her.

He didn't want to go first, but he didn't want Alison going first, either. Besides, he was the guy. When there might be danger, the guy is always supposed to lead the way.

He started down the cellar stairs, moving slowly. With the candle held out in front of his chest, he could see his feet and a couple of stairs below him. The bottom of the stairway and most of the cellar remained in darkness.

Alison was a single stair above him, but over to his right.

'This doesn't seem like such a good idea,' Mark whispered.

'It's fine,' Alison said. She put a hand on his shoulder. 'Don't worry.'

His legs felt weak and shaky, but he liked her hand.

We'll be okay, he told himself. I was down here all day and nothing happened.

Anything could be down here. Crouching at the foot of the stairs. Hiding *behind* them, ready to reach between the planks and grab his ankle.

We'll be fine, he told himself. Nobody's been killed in here in almost twenty years.

Says who?

At last, the shimmery yellow glow found the cellar's floor.

Nothing was crouched there, ready to spring.

Mark stepped onto the hard-packed dirt. Alison's hand remained on his shoulder as he walked straight toward the beast hole. When he came to the cordon, he stopped. Alison took her hand off his shoulder and stood beside him.

'How far in did you go?' she whispered.

'Pretty far. I don't know.'

'Want to show me where you found the glasses?'

'You mean go in?'

'Yeah.'

'Not really.'

'Come on.' She unhooked the cordon from its stanchion, let it fall to the dirt, then walked almost to the edge of the hole.

Mark followed her. 'We don't really want to go down there, do we?'

'I have to.'

'No, you don't.'

'You can wait up here if you want.'

'Oh, and let you go in alone?'

'No big deal.'

'It *is* a big deal. For one thing, it's awfully tight. I almost got stuck.'

'So stay here.'

'This is crazy.'

'If you say so.'

'It's just a stupid pair of glasses.'

'*Claudia's* glasses.'

'Even if they are . . .'

'Maybe *she's* down there, Mark. Maybe it's not just her glasses. I have to find out.'

'No, you don't. Anyway, she disappeared *months* ago. If she *is* down there, it'll just be her . . . you know, her body.'

'Whatever. Hold this.' She handed her candle to Mark, then began to unfasten the buttons of her denim jacket.

'You *don't* want to go down there.'

'Mark. Listen. Here's the thing. She knew.'

'Huh?'

'Claudia. She knew. She was always hanging on me. She was with me when a guy asked me out. Jim Lancaster. She heard me tell him the condition.'

The one condition.

I want you to get me into Beast House. That's where we'll have our date.

'Jim said I must be out of my mind,' she explained. 'No way would he try a stunt like that. So I told him he could forget about going out with me. After he went away, I said to Claudia, "Cute guy, but yella." '

'What did she say?'

Alison shrugged. 'I don't know.'

She turned away from the hole, took off her denim jacket, hung it over the top of the nearest stanchion and came back. The long-sleeved blouse she wore was white.

'Probably just laughed and said, "You're awful." Something like that. But this was only a week or so before she disappeared.' Looking into Mark's eyes, Alison slowly shook her head. 'Never even crossed my mind. She didn't run away to San Francisco. She came *here*. Just like you. To hide and stay till after closing time so she could let me in.'

'She didn't tell you anything?'

'She probably meant to sneak out later and surprise me. But I guess she never made it out.'

Chapter Eighteen

'Even if you're right,' Mark said, 'that's no reason to go *down* there.'

'It's my fault.'

'It is not. You didn't force her to do anything.'

'She did it for me. Now I've got to do this for her.' Alison bent over and peered down the hole.

'They might not even *be* Claudia's glasses.'

'They're hers.' She turned her head toward Mark. 'Are you coming with me?'

'If you go, I go.'

'Thanks.'

'You're gonna get filthy, you know. That white blouse.'

She glanced down at it, then looked at Mark.

Will she take it off?

'I didn't figure on crawling through dirt,' she said and looked toward her jacket.

'You can wear mine,' Mark said. 'It's already a mess.' He gave both candles to her, then unbuckled his belly pack, let it fall, and took off his windbreaker. She handed one of the candles back. He gave her the windbreaker.

'Thanks.' She poked the dark end of the candle into her mouth and kept it there, her head tilted back while she put on Mark's windbreaker and fastened it. When the zipper was up, she took the candle out of her mouth.

'Ready?' she asked.

'Not really.'

'Look, you stay here. I'll just go on down by myself.'

'No. Huh-uh. I'll go with you.'

'Just tell me how far in . . .'

'I don't know. Maybe twenty feet. Twenty-five?'

'Good. Wait here. It'll be a lot quicker that way, too. I'll just scurry in, have a look around. If I don't find anything, I'll come right out and we'll have plenty of time to do some exploring and stuff.'

'Well . . .'

'Anyway, you've already spent enough time down there. It's my turn.'

'I don't know . . .'

She sank to her knees. Looking over her shoulder, she said, 'You wait here, Mark. I'll be right back.'

'No, I'll . . .'

It came up fast, shiny white, almost human but hairless and snouted.

Alison was still looking at Mark and didn't see it.

But her face changed when she saw the look on his face.

Before he could shout a warning, before he had a chance to move, the thing grabbed the front of the windbreaker midway up Alison's chest and jerked her forward off her knees. She cried out. The candle fell from her hand. Head first, she plunged into the hole as if sucked down it. In an instant, she was gone to her waist.

Mark dropped his candle and threw himself at her kicking legs.

The flame lasted long enough for him to see that she was gone nearly to the knees. Then his body slammed the dirt floor. His head was between her knees and he clutched both her legs and hugged them to his shoulders as blackness clamped down on the cellar.

Gotcha!

Down in the hole, she was squealing, '*No! Let me go! Leave me alone! Oh, my God! Mark! Don't let it get . . .*' Then she yelled, '*Yawww!*'

Though Mark still clutched the jeans to his shoulders, he felt sliding movements inside them. He tightened his grip. The jeans stayed, but Alison kept going. Under the denim, her legs tapered. He felt her ankles. Then her sneakers were in his face and then they came off and fell away and he lay there hanging over the edge of the hole with Alison's empty jeans in his hands.

'*Alison!*' he yelled into the blackness.

'*Mark! Hellllp!*'

He pulled her jeans up, flung them aside, then squirmed forward over the edge and skidded down through the opening on his belly.

He bumped into her sneakers, shoved them out of the way, and scurried toward the sounds of Alison sobbing and yelping with pain and blurting, '*Let me go! Please! It hurts! Don't.*'

Mark wanted to call out and tell her it would be all right. Even if it was a lie, it might give her hope.

But he kept silent. Why let the beast know he was coming?

Maybe I can take it by surprise.

And do what?

He didn't know. But staying quiet made sense. It might give him *some* advantage.

Though he scrambled through the tunnel as fast as he could, the sounds from Alison seemed to be diminishing. She continued to cry and yell, but the sounds came from farther away.

How can they be faster than me? he thought. It's *dragging* her.

Though his eyes saw only utter blackness, his mind saw Alison skidding along through the narrow tube of dirt, on her back now, kicking her bare legs. The beast no longer dragged her by the front of the windbreaker;

now, she was being pulled by her arms. Stretched as she was, the windbreaker didn't even reach down to her waist. From her belly down, she was bare except for her panties.

It must really hurt, he thought. It must *burn*. Like rug burn, but worse, her skin getting scuffed off.

That'll be the least of her problems. When the beast gets done dragging her . . .

That's when I can catch up.

Yeah, right. And get myself killed. It'll take care of me in about two seconds.

But maybe those couple of seconds would give Alison a chance to get away.

It'll be worth it if I can save her.

Worth dying for?

Yeah. Fucking-A right, if I can save her.

Anyway, he told himself, you never know. It might not come to that. Anything can happen.

One of his hands slid over something slippery in the dirt. Her panties? The way she was being dragged, she'd been sure to lose them. Mark snatched up the skimpy garment, stuffed it inside his shirt and kept on scrambling forward.

The sounds from Alison seemed farther away than ever.

He tried to pick up speed.

What if they lose me?

133

According to the books and movies, there might be a network of tunnels behind Beast House, going all the way out past its fence and into the hills.

What if it really is some sort of maze?

The thing drags her off into side tunnels and loses me, I might have a chance of living through the night.

So far, the tunnel seemed mostly straight but with minor bends and slopes sometimes. If other tunnels had intersected with it, Mark hadn't noticed.

Though the sounds were far away, they still seemed to come from in front of him.

That's a good sign, he thought.

Sure it is. Good for who?

And a voice whispered in his mind, *I don't have to keep going. I can stop right now. Turn around and go back to the cellar and get the hell out. Let the cops take care of it.*

Better yet, don't tell anyone. Nobody has to know about any of this.

'Yeah, right,' he muttered.

And kept on through the darkness, out of breath, heart thundering, every muscle aching, his clothes clinging with sweat, his hair plastered to his scalp, sweat running down his face.

I can't keep this up forever, he thought.

So quit. That's what you want to do.

I don't want to quit, just slow down.

He stopped.

Just for a second.

Lying on his belly, head up, elbows planted in the dirt, he wheezed for air and blinked sweat out of his eyes and gazed into the blackness.

He couldn't hear Alison anymore.

It doesn't mean I lost her, he told himself. Maybe she stopped crying and yelling. Maybe she passed out.

In his mind, he saw her stretched out limp on her back, being dragged by her wrists, the windbreaker even higher than before so that she is bare from the midriff down. Her panties are gone. Mark can see between her thighs. Her legs bounce as she is dragged over the rough dirt of the tunnel floor.

'ALISON!' he shouted.

No answer came.

Chapter Nineteen

Mark wished he hadn't yelled. His shout had probably carried through the whole length of the tunnel.

I can't hear them, he thought, so maybe they didn't hear me.

What if they're just being quiet?

And it *heard me.*

In his mind, he saw the beast slither over Alison's limp body and come scurrying back through the tunnel.

Get the hell out!

He shoved himself up to his hands and knees, but the back of his head struck the dirt ceiling. He dropped flat.

Even if he *could* turn himself around, he knew he had no chance of out-racing the beast.

It'll be on me any second!

He listened. Silence except for his own heartbeat and gasping.

He would never see it coming. Not down here. Even something dead white would be invisible in such darkness. But he would hear its doglike snuffs and growls.

So far, he heard only himself.

What if it's still dragging Alison and they're getting farther and farther away?

Mark started squirming forward again.

Might as well, he thought. If it's coming, it'll get me anyway.

He picked up speed.

Get it over with.

In his mind, he saw himself and the beast scurrying straight toward each other through the tight tunnel like a couple of locomotives.

It's a locomotive, he thought. *I'm* a dog on the tracks.

He remembered the dog on the roof of the gift shop. Disembowelled and headless.

Is that how I'll end up? Or Alison?

As the tunnel began sloping upward, he wondered what was taking the beast so long.

Should've gotten here by now.

Maybe it *isn't* coming.

He struggled up the incline. All his muscles ached and trembled. His clothes felt soaked. Sweat poured down his face, stung his eyes.

And he saw gray.

Not actual light, but a hint of darkness that wasn't totally black.

He made his way toward it, shoving with his elbows

and knees and the toes of his shoes at the hard dirt floor of the tunnel and forcing himself forward, higher, closer to the gray.

Then he noticed a breath of air that smelled like fog and sea, that cooled the sweat on his face.

A way out?

That's why he'd stopped hearing Alison. That's why the beast hadn't come to get him . . . it hadn't heard his shout.

They aren't in the tunnel anymore!

And now the gray tunnel in front of Mark seemed to slant straight up. He tried to climb it, skidded backward, then got to his feet. Standing, he reached up and found rough, cool surfaces of rock.

He found handholds and started to climb. Soon, he was surrounded by large blocks of stone. Surrounded *and* covered. Looking up, he couldn't see the sky. But he did see a patch of pale, misty light from an area eight or ten feet above his head.

He climbed toward it, moving as fast as he dared up the craggy wall.

Hard to believe that the beast had made such an ascent dragging – or carrying – Alison. But it had some-how dragged her with great speed through the entire length of the tunnel. If it was capable of that, he supposed it could do this.

Boosting himself over a rough edge, he found the

opening in front of him. Not much. The size of a small window. But big enough.

He clambered toward it.

Beyond it, the night looked pale and fuzzy. Moonlit fog?

He crouched just inside the opening and peered out. Through the fog, he could see an upward slope of ground and he knew where he was; at the back of a rock outcropping just beyond the Beast House fence, a short distance up the hillside. He'd seen it many times. Never from the inside, though. Until now.

Outside, trees and rocks looked soft and blurry.

Nothing moved.

Where *are* they?

He stood up and saw the beast behind a thicket off to the left. Just its head and back, nearly invisible in the fog. It was hunched over as if busy with someone out of sight on the ground.

Mark crouched. Head down, he searched the area near his feet and found a good chunk of rock. It filled his hand. It felt heavy and had rough edges. Keeping it, he stayed low and hurried in the direction of the beast.

He didn't try to look at it again. If he could see it, it could see him. But he knew where it was. And he listened.

His shoes made hardly any noise at all as he hurried over the rocks and the long damp grass. The night seemed oddly still. All the usual sounds were muffled by the fog. Somewhere, an owl hooted. From far away came the low, lonely tones of a fog horn. He thought he could hear the distant surf, but wasn't sure.

Turning his head to the left, he looked downward and saw the back fence of Beast House with its row of iron spikes. Beyond the fence, there was only fog. Beast House was there, buried somewhere in the grayness. As he tried to glimpse it, he heard a snuffling sound.

Then a whimper.

He hurried on.

The sounds became more distinct. Moans and growls, panting sounds, whimpers and sharp outcries.

Some came from Alison.

She's alive!

But, oh, God, what's the damn thing doing to her?

Though Mark knew he must be very close to them, they remained out of sight. The beast had chosen a very well-concealed place for his session with Alison. It seemed completely surrounded by thickets and boulders.

Mark climbed a waist-high rock and looked down at them.

The monster, white as a snowman in the moonlit fog, was down on its knees, hunkered over Alison's back, thrusting into her. Her clothes were gone, scattered nearby. She still wore her white socks, but nothing else.

141

She was on her knees, drooping forward. She looked as if she would fall on her face except for the creature's hands that seemed to be clutching her breasts. Each time it rammed into Alison, her entire body shook and she made a noise like a dog getting kicked.

Mark leaped off the boulder.

The beast turned its head. Its eyes found him, but they didn't go wide with surprise. They stayed half shut. The beast seemed blasé about this human running toward it with an upraised rock.

But it very quickly stood up, still embedded in Alison, hoisting her off her knees and swiveling, letting go of her breasts and clutching her hips as she swung so that her head and torso swept downward and crashed against Mark, knocking him off his feet.

He slammed against the ground, rocks pounding his buttocks and back, one bashing his head. He heard the *thonk!* Felt a blast inside his skull. Saw bright red. Smelled something tinny like blood. Barely conscious, he gazed up at Alison.

She loomed above him. The beast's long, clawed fingers were clutching the sides of her ribcage, holding her like a life-sized, beautiful doll, working her forward and back.

Her chest and belly were striped with scratches, with gouges. Wetness fell off her and pattered onto Mark.

Her arms hung down as if reaching for him. But they

weren't reaching, they were limp and swinging. Her head wobbled. Her hair, hanging down her brow and cheeks, swayed with the motions of her body. Her small breasts, nipples pointing down at Mark, jiggled and shook as the beast jerked her forward and back.

She sniffled and sobbed. She let out a hurt yelp each time the beast jerked her toward it, plunging in deeper.

Mark raised his head.

The beast kept on working Alison.

Mark couldn't see much of it. Just its hands with their long white fingers and dark claws clamping both sides of Alison's ribcage. And its muscular white legs between Alison's legs.

Alison's legs were dangling, her feet off the ground. They gave a little lurch each time the beast rammed in. Through her sobbing and yelps and the beast's grunting, Mark could hear her buttocks smacking against the creature.

Smacking faster and faster.

The beast, grunting with each thrust, worked her forward and backward with increasing speed and power. Alison's arms and legs flopped about. Her hair swung. Her breasts lurched. Her yelps came faster.

It's killing her!

Mark's hands were empty. He turned his head and saw rocks nearby. He stretched his arm out and grabbed one and brought it closer to his side.

Above him, Alison's head flew backward. Mark thought the beast had tugged her hair, but its hands remained on her ribcage as it furiously slammed into her. Her head stayed back. Her mouth gaped. She gasped, '*AH-AH-AH!*' And then her arms stopped flapping. They bent at the elbows and she clutched her own leaping breasts and massaged them, squeezed them, tugged her nipples.

Chapter Twenty

What's she doing?

Mark *knew* what she was doing. Appalled, excited, he watched her growing frenzy.

All wrong, he thought. So wrong.

When the beast came, Alison's whole body twitched and bounced and she cried out and Mark was pretty sure she was having a climax of her own.

For a while afterward, the beast kept her in position. Her head and arms and legs hung limp. She hardly moved at all except to pant for breath. Then the creature eased her forward and upward. Its thick shaft appeared between her legs, and Mark saw it slide out of her.

Bending over, the beast lowered Alison toward him.

Does it think I'm dead?

Mark lay perfectly still as it put Alison on top of him. Her chest, hot and wet and heaving, covered his face. Hardly able to breathe, he turned his head to the side.

And waited.

Nothing happened.

Alison stayed on top of him, done in as if she'd just finished running a mile-long gauntlet.

But the beast did nothing.

What's it doing, watching us?

Just play dead, Mark told himself. If I make any sort of move at all, it'll probably drag Alison off me and rip me apart.

Though her moisture had soaked through Mark's shirt almost immediately, he soon felt a heavy warmth spreading out near his waist. It seemed to come from Alison, from between her legs.

My God, she's bleeding to death!

But the fluid felt thicker than blood.

Mark suddenly knew what it was.

It spread over his belly, rolled down his sides, soaked through his jeans so he could feel its warmth on his leg.

Must be a gallon of it.

As he lay there motionless, the night air turned the semen chilly. But it still felt warm where Alison's body was on top of him.

How long had she been there? Five minutes? Ten? Maybe longer. During that time, Mark had seen and heard nothing from the beast.

He felt Alison raise herself slightly.

'Don't move,' he whispered.

'Huh?'

'Play dead.'

'But it's gone.'

'Huh?'

'It went away . . . a long time ago.' Trembling, she scooted herself down Mark's body. She flinched and made hurt sounds. She said, 'Ugh.' Then her face was above his, her hair hanging toward him much as it had done when she was higher above him in the clutches of the beast. Now, however, she was nearly motionless and her hair hardly moved at all. He wished he could see her face, but it was masked by shadow.

'You came after me,' she said.

'Didn't do much good.'

'You tried.'

Her head slowly lowered. It tilted slightly to the side. She whispered, 'Thank you.' Then her mouth pushed softly against his mouth. Her lips were warm and wet and open.

We need to get away, Mark thought. It might come back.

But Alison was on top of him and kissing him and naked. He didn't want *that* to stop. He could feel her breasts through the damp front of his shirt. He could feel her ribcage and belly and groin and he was growing hard inside his wet jeans.

She lifted her face.

'We'd better get out of here,' Mark whispered. 'It might come back.'

'Don't worry.' Sitting on him, her buttocks on the soaked front of his jeans and heavy on his erection, she leaned forward and began to unbutton his shirt.

'What're you doing?'

She spread his shirt open, then eased herself down. Almost on top of him, she paused and swayed, brushing her nipples against his chest. Then she sank onto him, smooth and bare all the way down to Mark's waist. Her skin felt chilly at first, then warm. She kissed him again.

Has she lost her mind?

But the feel of her . . .

This was what Mark had always wanted, to have her like this, naked and eager. And how great to have it happening in the tall damp grass of a hillside late at night in the silence and the fog!

She pushed herself up.

'We've gotta go,' Mark said.

She started scooting backward. 'What's the hurry?'

'It'll come back and kill us.'

'I don't think so.'

'It *will*!'

'Why would it do that?'

'It's the *beast*!'

A corner of Alison's mouth curled up. 'If it wanted to kill us, why didn't it?'

'I don't know.'

'Neither do I,' she said. Squatting over Mark's thighs, she bent down and unbuckled his belt. 'But here we are, and it's gone.'

He pushed himself up to his elbows and looked around. The hillside and boulders and trees looked soft in the pale fog.

'It's gone,' Alison said again. She unbuttoned the waistband of his jeans, pulled down the zipper.

Some of Mark's tightness eased.

I can't believe this is happening.

'Maybe it got what it wanted,' Alison said. Scuttling backward on her knees, she tugged at Mark's jeans. He raised his rump off the ground. His jeans and underwear slid out from under him.

He was free and rigid in the moist night air.

'Now it's our turn,' Alison told him.

'But it *raped* you! It . . . it dragged you away and . . . look at you, you're all scratched and torn up . . . It . . . it *fucked* you!'

'It sure did,' she said. Crawling over him, she whispered, 'And we never breathe a word about this to anyone.'

'We've got to! You're all ruined!'

'I'll heal.'

'We've *gotta* tell.'

'Never. It'll be our secret. Just between you and me. *Everything* about tonight. Promise.'

Mark shook his head.

'Do you want me?' she whispered.

He nodded.

'Then promise.'

'But . . .'

She eased down and he felt a soft wet opening push against the head of his erection. It nudged him. He felt himself go in half an inch. Then she withdrew.

'Promise me, Mark.'

'What'll you tell your parents?'

'Nothing.'

'But you're all messed up.'

'Most of it won't show when my clothes are on. If they notice anything, I'll say I crashed my bike.'

'But . . .'

'Promise?'

'Okay.'

'Cross your heart and hope to die?'

'Yes.'

'Cross mine.' She moved forward and down so her chest was above his mouth. 'Use your tongue.'

He licked an X on the skin of her chest, tasting sweat and blood, feeling the furrows of scratches.

'Hope to die?' she asked.

'Yes.'

'Okay then.' She eased herself down and backward

and Mark felt himself slide in. She was warm in there. Warm and slippery and snug.

He knew the beast had been in before him, plundering her, flooding her. He'd heard crude guys talk about 'sloppy seconds' and he guessed that was what he was getting but he didn't mind very much.

Didn't mind at all, come to think of it.

Chapter Twenty-one

Near dawn, wearing what remained of their clothes, they made their way down the hillside. They stayed just outside the back fence and followed it. Alison could hardly walk. Mark held her. Sometimes, he picked her up and carried her for a while.

They came out of the field near some homes. Except for a few porch lights, nearly all the houses were dark.

They saw a cat. Once, a car went by a block away and they hid behind a tree. They saw no people anywhere. Only each other.

Soon, they arrived at Alison's house. All the windows were dark. So was the porch.

'I left the back door unlocked,' she whispered.

They went around the house. On the stoop outside the back door, Alison took off Mark's windbreaker and gave it back to him. Her white shirt was tattered, one sleeve missing and her right breast poking out through a split. Her legs were bare all the way down to her white socks.

'Are you sure you'll be all right?' Mark whispered.

'Pretty sure.'

He put on his windbreaker and zipped it up.

'Nice and warm?' Alison asked.

'Yeah.'

'I'm freezing.'

'You'd better go inside.'

'Not yet.' She took his hand and placed it on her naked breast. 'That's better.'

'Yeah.'

She held his hand there and whispered, 'I had a great time tonight, Mark.'

'You *did*?'

'Well . . . it had its ups and downs.'

'Jeez.'

She laughed softly, winced, then stared through the darkness at him. 'It *was* great.'

He felt goosebumps crawl up his body, but wasn't sure why.

'We'll have to do it again sometime,' she said.

'You mean . . .?'

'Go out together. You know.' She pressed his hand more tightly against her breast. 'You want to, don't you?'

'My God. Sure I do. Of course.'

'Me, too.'

Then Mark laughed softly and whispered, 'No conditions next time, right?'

'Only one.'